With all due respect,

for Spenser and Travis McGee -

two of the greatest.

Runaway

Flagg Mountain Press
13 Louisburg Square
Centerville, MA 02632

© Copyright 1996 by R. Pease

ISBN 1-889455-00-8

1

The phone rang. My digital clock read 0347. Flo turned over beside me. She was awake. She knew that only three people had my unlisted number. Even she didn't know what it was.

I lifted the instrument and put the receiver to my ear without saying anything.

"Jeeter? Are you there?"

It was Linda. Linda, who had walked out on me many years before, who hadn't been able to take the irregular precarious kind of life I led, a woman for whom I had never stopped caring.

"What is it, Linda?" I asked. Flo's warm hip was pressed against mine. She was listening.

"It's Speedy, Jeeter." Her voice was high and tense. "He's gone."

Speedy was one of the two boys Linda and Jonah had. He was the younger, about fourteen by now. Andy was two years older, if I remembered correctly.

"Tell me what happened," I said.

"Please come..." she started to say, but evidently the phone had been taken out of her hands.

"There's no need for you to come here. We'll handle this ourselves. You understand?"

"Jonah, listen a minute. I..."

"No. You listen. An' get it straight. We'll handle this ourself." And the line went dead.

I returned the phone to the cradle and lay back. Flo put her hand on my chest, waiting.

"You heard it all," I said. "Their younger boy, Speedy, has taken off. 'Gone,' Linda said. She was going to ask me to come over and Jonah took the phone away from her and said to stay put."

"You'll be going anyway, won't you."

"Yes. Can you understand?"

"You loved her once. That doesn't just stop. With you there's a kind of loyalty involved. She called for help. You'll go. I don't feel threatened. I only hope you won't get caught in the middle."

2

By five-thirty I was ringing the bell on the brick building in Roxbury where Linda and Jonah lived. Jonah bought the building two years before he met Linda. He'd improved it and maintained it so that it was the cleanest, best-kept house on the block. He and Linda were proud of their home. It was in both their names and they owned it free and clear now. It had doubled in value and doubled again in recent years.

There were lights on at the basement level where the kitchen was. I could see them shining at the end of the hall when I looked through the sidelights by the front door.

Jonah came up from below and along the corridor and opened the door. He was half a foot taller than I and sixty pounds heavier. For some twenty years he'd worked outdoors, a welder, one of those half-man, half-gorilla-people who put together the steel skeletons of skyscrapers. Balance and cunning and power and speed all essential, or he never would have survived.

"I told you we didn't need you," he said. He filled the doorway, arms at his sides, fists loosely folded.

Linda came up behind him and put both hands on his upper left arm. "Please, J. J." she said. "He can help us. Let him. For me?"

The hair on his head was all pointy on top and matted on the sides. Maybe he'd lain down for an hour earlier in the night, but mostly he'd been up, pacing, arguing, drinking cup after cup of coffee until he had a wild and caged look. He was wearing an old workshirt that hung outside his pants making him seem even broader than he was.

He turned his shaggy head to peer down into Linda's upturned face. Then he reached his right arm across his chest and gently held her against him. "All right," he said.

"Come on downstairs," he told me, as the two of them led the way along the hall.

I came inside and closed the door behind me. I'd been in their home maybe eight times over the years. Woodwork had been stripped of layers and layers of old paint and afterwards given two or three coats of spar varnish - hundreds of hours of loving work in order to bring forth the warm orange beauty of fir and the ruddy, fine-grained texture of mahogany.

The staircase to the basement level curved and rested on quarry tiles that Jonah had painstakingly installed over eleven inches of poured concrete. No rats would ever get into that house again - at least not from below.

Jonah rocked and paced and glowered at me from in front of the small kitchen fireplace. He had never trusted me. The two years that Linda and I lived together before he met her and took her away from me still rankled. He was jealous of the closeness we had known and looked on me as a rival, even now. He kept a grip on himself because he understood that if he ever tried to hurt me it would upset what he and Linda shared, but he was like a big bomb waiting to be detonated, a dynamite cap that only needed to be tapped one time.

For my part, I liked him. He was one of the most honest men I have ever known. Incapable of deceit, he lived by rules that were certainly too simple in a world such as ours, but what he believed guided him, and nothing could make him do what he thought was wrong. Also, he had given Linda security and a home and two boys - the things she had craved and that I still could not have provided.

Linda brought two cups of coffee to the heavy oval oaken table where I sat, one for her and one for me. Jonah had a cup on the counter top.

Gleaming, copper-bottomed pans hung from steam pipes near the ceiling. Pots of African violets perched on the window sills. The brick walls on all sides were painted off-white - more of Jonah's labors, pulling down old lath and plaster, scraping, pointing, filling chinks and gaps, then priming and painting.

Linda leaned toward me across the table. Salt tracks of dried tears marked her cheeks. Hair in disarray, wearing an old frazzled sweater over a torn blouse, she was still as lovely as ever. Almost forty now, she had put on only a few pounds. They lent her a greater maturity. Her coffee-bean-colored skin was still smooth and unblemished, always would be.

"He just put what he wanted to take with him in a shopping bag and left," she said. "He had on a tight deerskin jacket we gave him last Christmas. It zips up the front. He had a green wool shirt under it. Jeans. Old sneakers. Gray ones. No hat. No gloves."

She was seeing him over again, wanting me to see him too.

"The door to his room was open and I stood in it and watched him. 'What are you doing?' I asked him. But he wouldn't answer. He put underwear and socks into the bag, a baseball mitt and the fly ball he caught last summer that Wade Boggs hit into the stands where he was sitting and which Wade autographed for him later. I don't know if he had any money. I..."

She choked up and her eyes overflowed. She put both hands over her face so that only the tip of her nose was showing.

Jonah stepped to her and put his huge paws on her shoulders. He ground his teeth as he looked at me. He needed someone to blame for the pain Linda was feeling but he was too fair-minded not to know it was mostly helpless frustration that made him want to strike out at me.

"Was it last evening this happened?" I asked.

"It was yesterday afternoon," Linda said. "Jonah was still at work. Speedy came home when he should still have been in school. I could tell something was wrong. He went up to his room. I followed him."

"And when he'd taken what he wanted he just walked out?"

"He never said a word to me. He looked at me and didn't see me. He was a stranger. He was someone I had never met walking around in the body of my child. I must have started crying them. I've hardly stopped. I'm sorry. I don't know what I said to him. I'm sure I asked him what was the matter. Where he thought he was going. What I had done to him, or not done. Or given, or not given. I wanted to take him in my arms the way I always used to. But he's not a little boy anymore and I could tell he hated any hint of clinging. There was a wall of glass between us and he looked through it at me the way he would have looked at a person selling tickets at the movies or in the subway.

"He went down the stairs and I followed him, crying. He stopped by the table in the front hall and took something out of his pocket and put it beside the two candles there. He still hadn't said a word to me. Then he went out and shut the door behind him and walked to the corner. I looked to see what he'd put on the table. It was his key to the front door."

3

"Don't worry, Baby," Jonah said. He stood behind her kneading the good muscles of her shoulders and upper back, his voice a tender rumble. "He'll be comin' back. You'll see. He ain't but just a little kid. Got mad at me and took it out on you. He'll be comin' back, his tail between his legs. You'll see."

She reached one hand up to touch his fingers where they moved on her. They were together in their concern for each other. He was hurting too. He was already admitting that some of the responsibility for Speedy's leaving rested with him and Linda knew what it cost him to say so.

"How long do you think he's been planning on this?" I asked.

"I don't know," Linda said. "For a year or more now he's been acting different. It was just part of growing up, or adolescence, I thought. Andy was difficult too, still is. But Speedy has been impossible. No matter what we've expected of him he's done the opposite. He seemed to resent us and everything we've tried to do for him."

"Did he ever walk out before?"

"No. Well, sometimes when he was much younger and he'd have a fight with Andy he'd say, 'I'm gonna go away and never come back.' But it was just little boy talk. It didn't mean anything."

"Does he still...was he still having fights with his brother?"

"They went through periods when they were both small when they fought a lot. In the last few years, though, they seemed to be growing apart. You think that your children are going to love each other, be friends, play together and help each other, and instead they're like enemies. You see hatred in their eyes. What happens to make it turn out that way?"

I didn't have any answer to that one. "Jonah," I said, "do you think either of the boys has been fooling around with drugs?"

"No way," he said. "I'd know in a minute if any kid of mine ever tried anything."

I'd heard that before. Too often it's the parents who are the last to admit it, just possibly the last to know.

"What about in this last year when you say there's been a change, has there been some big thing you've disagreed about? Is there something Speedy wanted that you wouldn't give him? Or couldn't?"

Linda looked up at Jonah and waited for him to answer. He took his hands from her shoulders and slowly smacked his huge right fist into his left palm. "Maybe I been too hard on him," he said. It was something he hadn't wanted to say. Not to me. Not to Linda. I could guess how he had believed in laying down the law for his boys, how he had been a strict disciplinarian, what sort of obedience he had expected. It had probably been what he had known from his father once, so why shouldn't it have worked for his own children? Maybe for Andy it had.

"Did he ever stay away overnight before?" I asked.

"Not without letting us know where he'd be." It was Linda who had answered.

"Don't you think he'll come back today? Or tonight?"

"You don't know how stubborn he can be." she said. "Once he's made up his mind to something he never gives in. When he put his door key down on the front table I knew we had lost him."

She was about to start crying again. "He had to have somewhere he was going," I said. "Can you think of where?"

They looked at each other. How could they imagine anyplace Speedy would want to go? His home was with them. I could see the incomprehension in their faces.

"He's so young," Linda said, turning back toward me. "So many bad things can happen to him and he has no defenses. He's hardly more than a child."

In the alleyway behind the house someone was putting out trash cans. You could hear the thump and the scrape as one barrel was dropped against another. Then a gate banged shut and a moment later a back door went thlunk and it was quiet again, almost.

It was still dark in the city but traffic was already moving. Did it ever stop - the distant sound of sirens, the low mutter of trucks, subways, fire engines, cars starting up and driving away?

Where would a youngster go in the city, a black kid only fourteen, a willful headstrong boy who had never been on his own before?

"Find him for us, Jeeter," Linda begged. "Please find him for us."

4

The sergeant on duty at the district station was white and nearly sixty. He was studying a copy of *Hustler* and didn't look up when I came in. When I thought I'd waited long enough I said, "If it's not too much trouble, I want to report a missing person."

He glanced at me then, over the top of rimless bi-focals. "Maybe it is," he said. "Who are you?"

I showed him my ID.

"And licensed to carry," he said. "What is this world coming to?"

"Nice of you to ask," I said. "Do you really want to know, or will you tell me who takes this report?"

I think that for a moment he intended to say something uncomplimentary. Then he thought better of it, if thinking is the correct term for what went on in his head.

"Upstairs," he said, "and ask for Ashad, if he's there."

Ashad had a desk in a corner. He was young and black and his name had probably been Thomas or Brown or Jackson until recently. He was actually wearing a dashiki and from a fine gold chain around his neck hung a small polished bone. Reaching for his roots. The aboriginal missing person. Had they given him the job in jest?

He eyed me as I approached, sensing what was passing through my mind. It had happened before.

"Can I help you?" he asked. With one hand he motioned to the chair by his desk to indicate I could sit down if I wanted to.

"Thanks," I said. I handed him my ID. He looked at it carefully and made a note on a legal pad and handed it back.

"A young black male," I said. "Fourteen years old. Eric Johnson, known as 'Speedy.' He left home yesterday afternoon. I know," I said. "It hasn't been twenty-four hours yet and the parents need to come in themselves. They will. And they'll have photographs. I'm a close friend of the family and I'm going to do everything I can to help, but if this department can give any kind of assistance it will be greatly appreciated. And the sooner I get started, the better my chances."

"Do you know that a majority of the juveniles reported missing in this district come back home within twelve hours and that all but a few return within a week?"

"This one won't come home unless we find him. Not within a week. Maybe never."

"I've been told that a lot of times. What makes you so sure?"

"I know the boy," I said, "and I know the family. This is a very determined kid. And he's smart, too. He decided to take off. I don't know why yet and I don't know where he thought he'd get to. But he made a decision and he'll stick by it unless, or until, he finds out it was a bad one."

Ashad filled out forms. Linda and Jonah would come in later and provide answers to the questions I couldn't vouch for. It would all go on the teletype. I was given a phone number to call if I had information or if I located Speedy.

"The ones that don't come back get into trouble," Ashad said. "They go into crime or prostitution. The boys as often as the young girls. They wind up sick, or dead. A lot are never heard from again. Never found."

"What do you do to find them when you get a report?"

"What can we do? We set up one more file to add to the others."

"And that's it?"

"Just about."

"Have there been other reports of missing juveniles from this district lately?"

"Of course."

"Any kind of pattern to it?"

"Nothing I haven't seen week after week since I've been here."

"You seem resigned. As if there's not much to be done. As if there isn't even much use in looking."

"There isn't. The things the kids run away from don't run away. They stay right there. The old man who's a drunk. The mother who's a tramp. The house that's a dump without a father or a mother in it."

"But this boy has a beautiful home, parents who couldn't be nicer, an older brother who's doing everything right."

Ashad stared at me. He was at least fifteen years younger than I but he knew things I didn't know.

"Pressure," he said. "They've been pushing him. Gotta be as successful as his old man, as smart as his brother and as well-behaved, as neat and clean and beautiful as his mother. Gotta toe the line. Never be late to school. Come home before nine every evening.

"Fourteen, you said. They start pushing back hard by then. When nothing gives, they split."

I had the feeling he was right. "Are there many like that?" I asked.

"A minority among minorities," he said. He sounded bitter. Was he one of them?

"Could you give me a list of all those from this district who've taken off in the last few months?"

"What are you looking for?"

"Kids who were at the same school. Kids who lived in the same block. If Speedy was missing something at home he may have looked for it among other kids he knew. I might find two trails leading to the same place. Or three."

"Or a half dozen all going to different dead ends."

"Will you give me the list?"

"I can't. But I'll check it out for you. Call me late this afternoon. If I spot anything that looks helpful I'll tell you."

I stood up to go and held out my hand. He stood too and we shook. He was very tall, two thirds of it legs, and thin as a piece of wire.

"You grew up around here?" I asked.

"Just two blocks away."

"Will you be getting out?"

"I'll have a law degree in another year."

"If I ever need a lawyer I'll look you up."

"I'll leave an easy trail behind," he said, "so you won't have too much trouble finding me."

5

Speedy's school was an hour away from his home. Two hours of every day he spent going to and from when he had a neighborhood school he could have walked to. How much has busing cost us? How much good has it done? Flo says it's worth it no matter what the cost, the way to attack prejudice is to start with the children, you can hate all strangers, if that's your inclination, but you can't hate all your schoolmates.

There wasn't any busing when I went to school. Only three other black kids went to classes with me. We had a pretty rough time of it. But we made it. Jerry Frohock and I got to be pals early on. That tough skinny white kid and I found we could take on any combination of bullies in the school without having to give ground. After a while the others let us alone. Did Speedy gain as much by going to an 'integrated' school?

In the main office a woman shaped like a watermelon was typing out attendance slips. She frowned at me when I walked in. Maybe she thought I was looking for a job as janitor.

"Eric Johnson didn't show up today, did he?" I asked.

"May I ask what your interest is?" Real snotty.

"Sex," I said. "And murder."

"Very amusing. I'm afraid you'll have to come back later if that's what you're looking for."

"Maybe we should start over," I said. "Eric Johnson has left home. It doesn't look as if he intends to return. He is supposed to have been attending this school. Can you help?"

"I still need to know who you are and why you are interested."

"I'm a very close friend of the family. I'm also a private investigator." I showed her my license. "Now would you please tell me when Eric last came to school?"

Gracious acquiescence was never going to be one of her better qualities but she knew when she was licked. She got up and went to a filing cabinet and got out a card.

"Eric Johnson. Freshman. Age fourteen. Lives in Roxbury. No absences until October 19. In the month since then he's been absent eleven times. He is not here today."

She pushed the drawer shut as if that were the end of it with me.

"Could you give me the names of his teachers?" I asked.

"I have work to do and I don't have time for research. Also, I don't get paid for it."

I thought of offering her money but it didn't seem like a good idea.

"There's a kid on his own somewhere out there," I said. "He's almost certain to get into trouble, maybe he already is. If we can find him we may be able to help him. I won't ask you for anything else."

She was ready to sit down and start typing again but she hesitated. Then she turned to a different filing cabinet and got out a folder and told me the names of three teachers and what rooms they had. "You'll have to catch them between classes or at lunch time," she said.

I thanked her.

She looked at me. Some of the hostility was gone. "I hope you find him," she said.

6

Mrs. Bean had freshman English. I could imagine the fun the kids had with her name, but when I met her I was sure they never did it in her presence. She was built like a battleship and in the old days she would have been a knuckle-buster. Did they still use a ruler in the parochial schools, I wondered?

When the bell rang, the door to her room flew open and the students fled as if from a pit full of cobras. I had her all to myself. Lucky me.

"I really don't think I can help you," she said when I asked her about Eric.

She had one of those half-British accents you hear around Cambridge - affected and phony and full of its own omnipotent superiority.

On the blackboard behind her I read the words Respect, Discipline, Control, Infraction, Reprimand, Expulsion. Had I wandered into a cell block at MCI Walpole?

"He attended regularly until the middle of October," I said. "What sort of a student was he?"

"I would have to look up his grades in order to answer."

"Don't you remember? Isn't there some sort of impression he made on you?"

"I maintain my distance from the students at all times," she said. "Familiarity, as you know, breeds contempt. I do not collect impressions."

"You mean to say that you don't even remember the boy?"

"There are thirty-four students in this class and this is just one of three classes I have. Would you be capable of getting to 'know' each and every student if you were instructing that many?"

It was a fair question.

"I might not succeed," I said, "but I sure would try."

She wasn't going to be any help.

I got out of there and found the class in Western Civilisation where a Mr. Warren was supposed to be the teacher. The trouble there was that a substitute was in charge and as the bell rang it was obvious pandemonium would reign for the next fifty minutes.

The corridors emptied. I had one more name to pursue but it didn't look as if I was going to learn anything there either.

I wandered down the hall and took a stairway to the basement. A woodworking room was on my left. Farther on was a door marked BOYS, across from one marked GIRLS. The unmistakable sweet odor of pot reached me. How to get through the next boring class - light up, turn on.

A man even shorter than I, but three times as wide, was leaning against the door jamb to the Graphics room. He watched me as I approached but didn't say anything. He was wearing a tattered sweater that hung over rumpled pants. Maybe he was the guy who got the janitor's job.

"Morning," I said.

He sort of squinted. "You're not a new teacher," he said. "No more money for teachers. And you're a few weeks past the age of most students. So you want something."

"Maybe what I want you've got," I said.

"Try me."

"Do you know a boy who's a freshman this year, name of Eric Johnson?"

"Speedy?" The stub of a toothpick appeared in his mouth. His tongue maneuvered it the way a magician's fingers can turn a short pencil over and under his knuckles. I couldn't help watching it. "So you're a cop. What's Speedy wanted for?"

"Not wanted for anything I know of," I said, "except for running away from home."

"You a detective? No. They don't send out detectives after runaway black kids. You must be private. Am I right?"

"And I have a personal interest."

"You're his father."

"Not quite. I knew his mother years ago. I want to help find Speedy. I thought someone outside the family might know things about him his father and mother don't."

"They usually do."

"What can you tell me?"

"Let's go into the back room."

He led the way through a room full of offset presses, type presses and screen printing equipment to a cubicle that seemed to be his office. A name plate on the desk spelled out Costello.

"The Johnson kid is one of the quickest I've ever had in here," he said. "Never have to tell him anything twice. Show him how to do a thing and he has it. In Italy we used to say *capisce a volo* - understands in flight. I guess that's how he got the name Speedy.

"He was in here all the time. Bored silly in most of his classes. But even before I realized how smart he was, I knew he was up to something."

"Something illegal?"

"Illegal and tricky."

"Not printing money, I hope."

"They all think of that when they start coming here. No. Speedy is too sharp to fool around with anything that could put him in real trouble."

"So what was it?"

"This is only a guess. I never saw what he put together. But judging by the things he showed the most interest in, and some materials I think he must have taken, I'd say he was going to print some tickets."

I thought that over for a few minutes. Movie tickets could have saved him some change and might have gone unnoticed, but they were all in series and colors changed all the time. Sports events would be bigger and the tickets had to be distributed in advance - more chance to get an original and reproduce it. Still...

"Do you think he actually printed some?" I asked.

"I think he did."

"How long ago?"

"Two days ago. Speedy was here for fifth period. There was only one other kid in the room. I got called upstairs and was gone for half an hour. He wasn't around when I got back and I haven't seen him since. Now you tell me he's left home."

"You said maybe he took some materials. You mean equipment?"

"No, no equipment. I mean paper. There are two sheets of heavy stuff missing. A kind of cardboard. Beige. A dozen kids could have taken it. Speedy is not necessarily the thief. Or the one who spoiled it and threw it out. I wouldn't even have noticed it was gone, except that I'd ordered it special and needed it myself."

"Is there any left?"

"One sheet. You want a sample?"

I told him I'd appreciate it. We went back into the work room and he snipped off a piece of the stiff cardboard for me.

"Do you remember who the other student was who was alone here with Speedy two days ago?"

"Sure. It was MacCallister. A real quiet one. Intense. Not quick but a plugger. Sets himself a job to do and no matter what troubles he has he gets it done, even if it takes twice as long as it should. Erwin MacCallister. Why do parents give kids names like that? No wonder he keeps quiet."

"Will you be seeing him today?" I asked.

"Erwin? He'll be in last period."

"Would you ask him if he saw what Speedy was doing the other day? If he tells you, could you call it in to my answering service?" I gave him my card. "I'd like to find Speedy before he gets himself into a real jam."

Costello took my card and put it in his wallet. "I hope you can," he said. "What worries me about him is he's probably too smart for his own good."

7

The ticket agency in town covered just about every kind of event you could think of if it was going to draw a crowd and required a paid admittance - flower shows, ballgames, theater, concerts, fights, fundraisers.

Judging by the amount of heavy paper that had been taken from the Graphics Room, Speedy couldn't have made more than twenty to thirty tickets even if he didn't waste any. I couldn't see him going to plays or symphony concerts or a flower show and it didn't seem likely that he only wanted the price of admission. He was a baseball fan but that season was over now and football didn't interest him, according to his father. If larceny was his aim he might have...

I asked the lady in charge if there were any big events that were sold out.

"Tonight," she said. "At the Centrum, in Worcester. The Boss."

"Who is the Boss?" I asked.

"The Boss is Bruce Springsteen. Rock star. Where have you been all these years if you haven't heard of him?"

"I lead a sheltered life," I said. "Did you have tickets for his show?"

"We had a hundred. They sold out the first ten minutes we had them on sale."

"What would scalpers get for those tickets at the door tonight?"

"I wouldn't know."

"A wild guess."

"They could go as high as two hundred dollars each."

I got out the piece of cardboard Costello had given me and showed it to her. "Were the tickets printed on material about this color and weight?"

She took it in her hand and felt it and looked up at me. "Do you think someone may have printed phony tickets in order to sell them at the gate?"

"It looks like a real possibility."

"And a chance to get away with a bundle."

"Or to wind up in jail," I said.

8

I went back to my apartment on Revere Street and found Flo with an old scarf protecting her hair and a shapeless long linen dress covering the rest of her. She was cleaning. She'd pulled all the books out of the bookcases.

"You may be a nut about order," she said, "but did you ever hear about dusting?"

She sounded really angry. Maybe she was. There were big gray woolly dust rolls on every shelf behind where my books had been. And scraps of paper and gum wrappers had fallen back there too. A couple of pencils. Even some loose change.

Flo had moved in with me only a month earlier and her husband, Tom Porter, had never come after her. Perhaps he figured that any white woman who'd live with a black man wasn't worth chasing. Now here was Flo wrestling with my former ties to Linda.

"Guess you gonna give me a good whuppin'. That right, Momma?" I said.

She'd been building up to some kind of outburst.

"Is Linda just as pretty as ever?" she asked.

"She is."

"And you still love her?"

"That doesn't just stop, as you said yourself."

She remained standing, legs wide apart, two yards in front of me. "Do you deserve a good 'whuppin'?" she asked, trying to get the accent right and making the word sound foolish instead.

"Only for being a lousy housekeeper."

We both started to smile. Then there were tears in her eyes and she was laughing.

We were still new to each other. The ways of handling differences hadn't been worked out yet and jealousy was unexpected. How would I react if Tom Porter came back on the scene?

"I'm being stupid, aren't I," she said.

"Sort of. But I'd have been disappointed if you'd had no reaction. The phone rang in the middle of the night. It was Linda. I jumped out of bed and went flying to help her. I've been gone for seven or eight hours and you've had no way of knowing what I've been doing."

"What have you been doing?" Relaxed now, tears wiped away, leaning into my arms.

She was warm and soft against me. I held her close and kissed her. How many times in the last ten years had I returned to an empty apartment or motel room or rented room where no one waited and no one cared?

We went into the kitchen and got out the left-over avocado salad from the night before, and pumpernickel bread and brie and oranges while I told her about the morning.

She was a good listener and quick to put things together. When she asked a question it was always pertinent.

I told her about Linda and Jonah and how Speedy had packed and left, dropping his key to the front door on the entrance table. I told her about Ashad and the school and Costello and the ticket office.

"What about Speedy's brother, Andrew?" she asked. "You haven't spoken with him yet, have you?"

"I want to talk with him when his parents aren't around," I said. "I want to go back when Jonah isn't there and go through Speedy's room and ask Linda about both boys because I think she and Jonah have not agreed on how to raise their kids, but in Jonah's presence Linda won't speak out. Maybe none of that will be necessary, though. We may catch up with Speedy tonight."

"You think he'll be in Worcester?"

"It lookes that way. We'll see if Costello finds out anything from young MacCallister. He'll leave the message with my answering service sometime this afternoon. Unless it's negative, I thought you and I and Linda and Jonah might go to a rock concert tonight."

"We won't actually have to go to hear, will we?"

"If it costs two hundred dollars apiece to get in I doubt if any of us will think it's worth it."

"We'll be looking for Speedy, the scalper, in the crowd. Is that it?"

"And with four of us, if he's there, we have a good chance of spotting him."

"Do you think Linda and Jonah will come along? They may not want to believe their boy could be up to something crooked. Jonah may resent the suggestion."

"I expect he will."

"Can you handle him?"

"If Jonah ever lost his temper he could be very dangerous, but he's the kind of man who'll think first. In the presence of two women he won't start a fight. I don't mean to say I'll be hiding behind anyone's skirts. I mean that Jonah is a courteous man. Unless someone he cares for is threatened he'll control himself."

"And you want the four of us to travel all the way to Worcester and back in your little Toyota? Is that wise?"

"They don't have a car and they'll be the first ones to recognize their son. If he's there. The crowd will be a big one."

"For me it'll be awkward."

"I know."

"Why do you want me to come along? I don't have any idea what Speedy looks like."

"You don't have to come if you don't want to."

"Do you want me to?"

"Yes."

"You still haven't said why."

Why did I? So she wouldn't be left alone again wondering and worrying? So I could show her off? So she could meet Linda?

"Maybe it's because I think we belong together," I said.

We left the few dishes in the sink and went into the bedroom. We took off our clothes and made love in the sunlight that fell through the south window warming and dappling us, crosshatches of windowpane on our bodies and the unhurried gathering of pleasure a soft wind rising and lifting us.

9

I came up out of sleep and the short autumn afternoon was already turning dark. Flo was in the shower. I called my answering service. Costello had left a two-word message: "Surmise confirmed."

Linda answered on the first ring. "We'll be by to pick up you and Jonah at six," I said.

"You know where Speedy is?"

"I think we're going to find him in Worcester."

"What would he be doing there?"

"I'll explain everything when we come to get you."

"You say 'we.' Who will be with you?"

"I'm not alone anymore, Linda."

"You mean..." She hesitated. "I'm glad," she said at last.

"Listen," I said. "We're going to be looking for Speedy in a rock crowd. We want to spot him before he sees any of us. If possible. If you and Jonah can be wearing something Speedy hasn't seen before it should improve our chances."

"That won't be too difficult. Do you think he'll come back with us, if we find him?"

"That's another problem. Let's find him first. Please be sure to be ready at six."

10

There was a street light in front of their house. No place to park. But they must have been watching from a front window. Linda came out right away with Jonah close behind her. She was wearing tight black pants and an insulated blue jacket over a pink blouse. Her hair was done up tight, high on her head. She looked like a woman in her mid-twenties.

Jonah, immense, had on all dark clothes and a black leather jacket. He carried a shopping bag in his left hand. It contained something the size of a basketball.

I got out of the car as they came down the walk and Flo got out too. Jonah came to a halt when he saw Flo. He looked from her to me and back to her again and if he'd said it out loud - which he didn't - it wouldn't have been clearer. 'A gray broad,' he was thinking.

I made the introductions. Jonah was standing taller than usual, stiff, leaning backwards. Flo and Linda ignored him. I think something passed between them. They were studying each other but not in a cold or critical manner. They got into the rear of the car together and we pushed the passenger seat way back so Jonah's huge frame would fit in front next to me and I drove off.

Getting out of Roxbury and onto the Pike took some time and concentration. Traffic was extra heavy. It was a cold night but clear and a lot of people seemed to have decided to go out for the evening. Or maybe everyone was going to Worcester too.

"You gonna tell us where we goin' and how come?" Jonah asked after we got out of the city.

I told him about Ashad and Speedy's school and Costello and the ticket office. Linda and Flo were listening.

"So you want me to believe that from one day to the next my kid has turned into a crook?" He didn't like it. Why would he?

"Somebody could have put him up to it, Jonah. It could be a dare. Even if we find him and can talk with him we may not find out why he got involved in this. If he is involved."

"Maybe we just wastin' a lotta time goin' to Worcester and Speedy gonna be sittin' on the doorstep when we get home."

"I think we're going to find him passing out worthless tickets in return for big money and I hope we can stop him before he gets into serious trouble."

"I catch him sellin' worthless tickets, I bust his ass."

"J. J." Linda said, "if we find him, let's let him tell us his side of the story first."

He swung around in his seat and glared at her, looked again at Flo as if for confirmation of his first impression, and then turned back to stare into the traffic ahead of us.

It was like sitting next to a grizzly bear. His breath came in deep huffs and when he shifted position my small car rocked like a puff ball on a puddle. His forearm, resting on his knee next to the stick shift, was as thick as the upper part of my leg and from somewhere inside him came a low sound that was almost a growl.

"Take a damn good story to keep him from feelin' my hand if he doin' wrong."

I wondered if Jonah was trying to sound extra black for Flo's benefit. Or was I more aware of his speech becuase she was there? When she and I were together and no one else present I hardly ever thought of color anymore. I'm sure she didn't either. But right now she would be sitting there behind me acutely aware of differences and the countless sensitized areas where any inept word or gesture could be wrongly taken. Was Jonah warning her of the chip on his shoulder - the one we all carry?

"Maybe it's only a prank," Linda said. "Or a way of proving something to himself. Kids do these things."

"Not all kids," Jonah said.

"This one did," I said. "It wasn't a disaster. And no one batted me around to make me see the light."

"Whadya do? Steal a quaddah from your Maw?" He wasn't going to be easy to convince.

"Another kid and I started ripping off apartments in a section of Cambridge where there were all three-deckers."

Jonah turned to stare at me. The car rocked.

"You never told me that," Flo said.

I caught her eye in the rear view mirror. "I never told anyone before," I said.

Now it was my turn to get the full treatment of Jonah's triple-whammy look.

"So you just a goddamn crook after all," he said.

"You know I'm not, Jonah." I met his gaze and then had to give my attention to driving again.

"I was first year in high school. Like Speedy. I had a friend who was just as tired as I was of being told what to do all the time. It was a way to break one of the biggest rules of all. I don't think either one of us would have done anything alone. We needed to be sure that someone else knew what we had done."

"How long you keep it up?"

"We broke into three places. In the first, we took some jewelry which turned out to be colored glass. In the second, we found eighteen dollars. We got a wino to buy us a bottle of whisky with the money and we got drunk and then deathly sick. The third time, we watched an old couple leave their ground-floor apartment and go to a bingo game where they'd be busy for two or three hours. We went back to their place and pried open the window on the back porch. They had four rooms. The place was immaculate. There was certainly money hidden somewhere there and we could have found it, but all of a sudden neither one of us wanted it. We left the way we came in. We didn't take a thing."

A trailer truck came up behind us and passed doing over seventy miles an hour. We were whipped about by the change in air pressure around the car.

"So you never got caught."

"We never did."

"But you quit."

"Yes."

"You like some modern-day preacher, Jeeter. No hellfire and damnation. No sulfur and brimstone. Just some cutesy ol' made-up story to teach us the lesson. Am I right?"

"I didn't make it up, Jonah. It's the truth."

He wasn't going to say he believed me but he didn't answer. He turned toward the road once more and crossed his arms over his sequoia chest and didn't speak again until I found a place to park, half a mile away from the Centrum.

"We gonna split up and look for Speedy and meet back here. That the program, Boss?"

There was sarcasm in his voice but it was tempered.

"And if any one of us sees him we should try to signal the others," I said. "And remember. He's not going to like it if we find him."

I put on a pair of wrap-around dark glasses. Speedy might not remember me, even without them, with them, I knew he wouldn't recognize me.

Jonah opened the shopping bag he'd brought along. He got out of the car and put on a white crash helmet. It added another two inches to his height. With a badge and a night stick he would have looked like a one-man riot squad. No one was going to stand in his way. Not for long.

Also in the shopping bag was a blond wig. I think they call it a fall. Linda put it on along with a pair of shades. She looked as if she belonged on a street corner in the Combat zone. My consternation must have showed. Linda smiled. "Every woman wants to play the part at least once," she said.

"Speedy see us now," Jonah said, "he run away for good."

Flo had taken my arm. She wasn't smiling. Her expression was filled with anxiety. It took me a moment to understand. Of course. Here were all us darkies. Minstrel show about to begin. Couldn't wait to make fools of ourselves for the white audience. She was praying Jonah wouldn't see it that way.

About half an hour remained before Bruce was due to go on. We made our way through an increasingly dense crowd toward the main entrance. Mostly, it was teen-agers who had come, but there was an odd assortment of older persons, some obvious hustlers and deviates, a married couple here and there who still thought to belong, a few drunks, parents frenziedly pursuing children determined to escape.

Linda took off to my right, Jonah plowed into the middle, and Flo and I went left into the noisy, unruly mob. Presumably, Jonah could see where Linda went and all of us could make out Jonah's white helmet.

But there were others wearing helmets. A motorcycle gang had come in behind us. They looked like trouble but maybe I was simply prejudiced. In any case, none of them was as tall as Jonah.

People with tickets kept shoving forward to get in and others, without tickets, kept stopping them, offering to buy what they had. I hadn't spotted any scalpers yet. There were cops standing by. I assumed there were men in plain clothes among us in the crowd.

Then I saw Jonah turn our way and gesture over his left shoulder with his thumb before turning again and beginning to move toward the right of the main gate. Almost at the same moment a yell went up which turned into a roar.

"Go back to the car," I said to Flo, and began forcing my way in the direction I'd seen Jonah headed. Spreading through the mob like wildfire, was the word that someone had been selling fake tickets. If it was Speedy and the crowd got to him he could get killed.

Uniformed police were coming from all sides. From one minute to the next we were in the midst of a riot. Fights had broken out all over the place. I saw one teen-ager running for his life before he got tackled and a circle formed around him. Maybe Speedy hadn't been alone.

Thirty feet in front of me, Jonah lunged at a stocky middle-aged man who had his fist cocked to throw a punch. For a split second I caught sight of Speedy, the intended target. Jonah grabbed the man's arm and then at least five people piled onto his back. He lost his helmet and went down. I got to his side as a local cop raised his night stick to deliver a lethal blow to Jonah's skull.

There wasn't time to say anything. No one could have heard me anyway. I got a grip on the stick and pulled the cop over backwards. He let go and I lost my footing for half a second. I saw him reaching for what was probably a tube of mace. Someone shoved me toward him. I put a knee into his balls hard enough to make him wish he'd never had any and as he bent forward I rabbit-punched him so he collapsed on the ground. Speedy had vanished.

Jonah was getting to his feet. "Let's get out of here while we can," I said. More cops were headed our way. The crowd was thinning out. We kept our heads down and managed to merge with the stream of people leaving the area.

Linda was standing in the back of a pick-up truck. She saw us coming. She'd had a pretty good view of the whole scene. I didn't see Flo anywhere. Then I heard her call. She came up behind us from a row of parked cars. We got back to my Toyota and got in and drove away.

11

"He was still wearing the deerskin jacket we gave him," Linda said. "I was only a few feet away from him when he looked at me and frowned. He'd recognized me. Then that man in the plaid jacket was about to hit him and J. J. stopped him. Speedy seemed to sink into the ground and disappear. I don't know where he went."

We were back on the Pike. There was hardly any traffic. "There were three others," Flo said. "They all ducked and ran at the same time. One of them got caught and would have been beaten up but a man who seemed to have no neck saved him and he got away."

That must have been the kid I saw tackled. I hadn't seen anyone come to his rescue. "Do you suppose the man was his father?" I asked.

Flo had no idea. It didn't seem too likely. Perhaps, if there were four kids in on the scam, some adult had been their driver. If the others were Speedy's age none would have a driver's license - not a valid one.

"Did you get hurt any, J. J.?" Linda asked.

"Uh-uh," Jonah said, "but it was close." He looked at me. "That Worcester cop is gonna remember you."

"But he doesn't know where to look for me."

"The helmet I borrowed is back there."

"Does it have a name in it?"

"Sure does."

"Close friend of yours?"

"Close enough."

"Close enough to lie and say it got stolen a couple of days back in some logical place? Framingham maybe?"

"I'll make him understand."

"And I'll pay for the new helmet."

"No way. I owe you for more than the helmet. My whole skull would be more like it. That mother was about to turn my brains to jelly."

"He's the kind of cop who ought to get transferred to Sanitation."

"Already did," Jonah said. "After what you did to him, he gonna be using sanitary pads for the rest of his life." He laughed. The whole car shook. I saw Flo's face watching me in the rear view mirror. She was smiling. The tension was gone.

But Linda wasn't smiling. She was scrunched way back into the corner behind Jonah, hugging herself, her jaw clenched. "You and Speedy both could have been killed," she said. "And he's gone again. What crazy thing will he try next? Where do we start to look for him now?"

"If he's part of a group," I said, "he'll probably be in less danger than if he were on his own. Also, he should be easier to locate."

"But where do we start?"

"I was supposed to phone Ashad this afternoon. He may have something for me. I'll call him in the morning. And sometime in the day I'd like a chance to talk with Andy. When could I catch him when he and I can be alone?"

It was Jonah who answered. "Andy goes to the 'Y', one to three, every Saturday afternoon. You wait for him there, a few minutes to three, you catch him."

They were quiet after that. Flo hadn't spoken three times the whole evening. She'd been watching and listening - the trained observer. When I let Jonah and Linda off at their home Flo got back into the front seat beside me. We were almost back to Revere Street when she spoke. "Does anyone ever have children without being hurt?" she asked. She was thinking of her own child, born mongoloid, institutionalized. Was that any worse than having a normal child who runs away? Or was the worst thing of all never having any?

I found a place to park at the bottom of Garden Street and we walked up the Hill holding each other. The sky was down around the tops of the higher buildings. Night lights and night shadows followed us. The cold was like needles on our skin.

12

It was almost ten AM by the time I got to the station. Ashad was in his corner. He looked up as I approached his desk. "Thought you were going to phone," he said. He was wearing an old faded blue sweatshirt and black corduroy pants and running shoes.

"Have you got something for me?" I asked.

"Might have."

"Don't be coy."

"Hardly ever get the chance."

"You found another runaway Speedy may have known."

"Better. And worse."

The way he was looking at me I knew there was some bad news.

"Where were you last night?" he asked.

So that was it. I didn't like to lie to him, but he was a cop and he couldn't afford to withhold information - if he had it. "I was at home most of the evening," I said. "What does that have to do with Speedy?"

I think he knew that I wasn't leveling with him.

"Can anyone back you up?"

"No problem."

"I hope so," he said.

"How about telling me what you found out."

I picked a folder off the chair next to his desk and handed it to him and sat down. He put the folder on top of a pile in front of him.

"Another fourteen-year-old took off the same day Speedy did. Name is Leroy Willis. They went to school on the same bus. I put photos of both Leroy and Speedy on the teletype yesterday afternoon and we got a report back this morning. They were seen in Worcester last night. Both of them. And two other kids about the same age who just might turn out to be runaways too."

He was still looking at me with his eyes half closed. In this business you get so you can tell if someone you're talking with is concealing anything. There are signals you tune in to. Don't ask what they are. A few you might be able to identify, but mostly it's a feeling you get, a certainty that grows on you that the other person is not being truthful. Ashad knew I'd been in Worcester.

"All four were scalping tickets to a show at the Centrum. The tickets were phonies. At least nineteen outraged fans didn't get in after paying anywhere from one hundred and fifty to just under two hundred dollars for what should have given them admittance. We don't know how many others got in and could have been turned away. Those kids made off with well over four thousand dollars. They started a riot. Several people got hurt. And one Worcester cop says a black dude with wrap-around shades assaulted him when he was about to a make an arrest."

"An arrest of one of the kids?"

"That's what he claimed, but a patron who got clipped on a counterfeit ticket says the cop was about to brain a big black man who was lying on the ground when the dude with the shades took the club out of his hand."

"Sounds like a cop who gets his kicks beating up on minorities."

"It does, doesn't it."

"How's he doing, the cop that got his stick taken away?"

"Not too good. He's walking around bent over like a very old person. Apparently this mystery person, the runty black dude, put a knee into the cop's privates so that he's now on the disabled list."

"Must be tough, being a cop."

"Yeah," Ashad said. "Can be humiliating too."

"Can you give me the address of the other runaway, Leroy Willis?" I asked.

Ashad wrote street and number on a slip of paper and handed it to me. "We might get a make on two of the others," he said. "Phone me later today or tomorrow. I'll let you know."

I got up to go. "Thanks," I said.

"Better be looking over your shoulder for a while," Ashad said. "You never know who might be coming up behind you."

He didn't need to warn me. If I didn't have eyes in the back of my head I wouldn't still be alive. He probably knew that. It was just his way of saying I hadn't fooled him.

13

Leroy Willis lived one street away from Speedy. When I knocked on the front door the curtain in the window at my right was pulled back and an old seamed black face gave me a long look before disappearing and then reappearing in the crack where the door opened only as far as a chain allowed.

"Eric Johnson has run away from home," I said. "He and Leroy Willis know each other. If this is where Leroy lives I'd like to talk with you."

Her face didn't change expression. She was one of those old black ladies who have seen it all. Ageless and impassive, with dim watery eyes, they could have been around since the days of ancient Rome. Nothing surprises them. Frail but somehow formidable they endure where countless others live for a while and then die or disappear. She'd seen me and heard my voice. She knew me.

The door closed. The chain was taken off. The door swung wide. "Come in," she said.

She led the way into a front parlor filled with heavy Victorian furniture and photographs and knick-knacks and oil paintings. An upright piano stood against one wall, a piano stool with crystal feet before it. On the marble mantlepiece was a figure cast in bronze - Sojourner Truth, long striding, confident, determined.

I sat on a chair that had a fixed base on which the upper part rocked. The arm rests terminated in carved lions heads. The lady of the house sat by the window in a straight-backed wooden chair, her hands folded in her lap, waiting.

"Has Leroy run away too?" I asked.

"He's gone," she said. "He put what he needed in a backpack and told me goodbye. I asked him where he was going. He said not to worry. He said he needed to live. I didn't know what I could say to that."

"Are you his...?"

"I'm his grandmother. I had seven children. They all left this home long ago. Cinthy was the baby. She went down to New York City with a trumpet player when she was only nineteen years old and five years ago she came back and left Leroy with me. 'He'll be better off with you, Momma,' she said. She wouldn't tell me where she'd been all those years. She'd seen a lot of trouble. I could tell. She went away again and I've never had another word from her."

"Have your other children kept in touch?" I asked.

"Life sweeps us all away," she said. "Too much to do. Too many problems. Too little time. One of my girls is a teacher in New Haven. She writes me now and then but I never see her. Two of the boys got killed in the war - that war in Viet Nam. One son is in Saudi Arabia, an engineer, making lotsa money. He says he'll come to see me someday before I die. That would be nice. The others have families. Live far away. Must have forgotten how to write."

"And your husband?"

"Mr. Reese died long ago. He was diabetic. I pray for him each morning when I wake up and every night before I go to bed. Life had meaning when he was here. But he left me too. They've all left me now."

Was it self-pity she was feeling, the tainted emotion, the poor-me reflex many look on with such disdain? She'd outlasted half her family, done everything she could for every one, no doubt, had raised seven children to adulthood. Probably she'd been provider, too, after her husband died. Had she taught, to earn the money a large family required? One daughter had gone that route.

"The Lord giveth and the Lord taketh away," she said. There was nothing in the way she said it to indicate she had ever questioned divine wisdom, or its existence. She was not simply resigned. She believed.

I admired her strength. Perhaps I envied her her faith.

"What can you tell me about Leroy?" I asked.

She got to her feet, squared her thin shoulders, took a deep breath. "I'll show you his room...his 'partment,'" she said. It was the first time any local accent had been noticeable in her speech. She may have sensed my reaction.

"I had two years at Vassar," she said, "before Mr. Reese married me and I started having babies. My Daddy wanted me to grow up to be a lady. He said black people needed to make up for a lot of lost time and they should set every hurdle as high as it would go. His Daddy was a slave."

We had reached the hallway and were about to climb the stairs. She paused with one hand on the newel post.

"And you, Mr..."

"Jeeter. They call me Jeeter, Mrs. Reese."

Those old moist smoky eyes rested on me, not so much seeing as reaching into me. "You never finished school, did you, Mr. Jeeter."

"I dropped out when I was seventeen," I said. I wasn't going to tell her why.

She was still looking into me. I had the feeling that she could sense all that happened that year. Her face was a charcoal mask in which only the lips moved when she spoke. I had not seen her blink. She was a mind reader, a kind of medium, but her inborn gentility held her from putting words to that which might be painful.

She turned and went up the stairs ahead of me. "The top of the house is all closed off," she said, "full of things and memories, but I let Leroy have the whole second floor. He was the one who always said, 'This is my partment.' He didn't like me to clean it or straighten it up."

There was a front room and a rear room on the second floor with a walk-through closet in between. "This is the first time I've been up here since he left," Mrs. Reese said.

We entered the rear room where there was a big double bed, neatly made up. A marble-topped bureau stood against one wall. A floor lamp and an armchair and a very good oriental rug completed the furnishings.

"May I look through his things?" I asked.

"I think that would be all right," she said.

I went through the contents of the bureau. There was little there except socks and underwear and shirts, some sweaters in plastic bags. Everything was neat. Apparently a few items from each drawer had been taken when he left. The bottom drawer held much-used equipment and a battered rule book for the game of Dungeons and Dragons.

In the closet I found a basketball and a catcher's mitt. A winter coat that would have been too big for him hung there. A hand-me-down, no doubt. The same could be said for several other items - shirts and jackets. Mrs. Reese must have put them there, thinking Leroy would grow into them in time.

And the big front room that looked down on the street was almost as spare as the rest of the place. There was a desk by the window with school books on it. One wall had built-in bookselves and a considerable array of paperback science fiction filled several of them. A sofa. A portable TV. Some chairs. On one wall were pictures of Boston Celtics players - all the way from Bird back to Cousy. On another were photos of baseball stars - quite a few that I didn't recognize. But there was none of the clutter I would have expected from a teen-ager.

It was disquieting. A boy who was now an adolescent had lived here for five years, according to his grandmother, yet there was no accumulation of things once used or played with. Where were the train sets, the models, the electrical kits, the puzzles, the record player and rock music, the guitar with strings missing, piles of dirty clothes, a work-out mat, magazines - all the detritus, the junk, that youngsters always stack up where they live and won't let their elders touch? This was the retreat of a monk, not the lair of a fourteen-year-old. It was bare and cold and empty and I couldn't wait to leave it behind.

Mrs. Reese came with me to the door. We had hardly spoken while we were upstairs.

"Did Leroy have many friends?" I asked.

"Not that he ever told me about."

"How about Speedy Johnson?"

"Speedy used to come here once in a while. They went to school together. Sometimes they went to Fenway, to a ball game, just the two of them."

"The game of Dungeons and Dragons that's in the drawer of the bureau upstairs - it looks as if it's been used a lot. Did a group of boys play that together?"

"Week-ends, this fall, he went off with that game and played somewhere. He didn't tell me where, or with whom he played. I used to try to get him to talk with me about things but it was as if he didn't trust anyone anymore. Maybe he'd trusted his mother once. Or his father - if he ever knew him. He wasn't going to take that chance again, it seemed."

She touched my arm lightly. I imagine she had wanted contact with Leroy too, but that he had drawn away from her. "I hope you can find both boys," she said. "I hope they haven't come to any harm."

14

At a couple of minutes after three Andy came out of the Y. How long had it been since I'd seen him last? A year? Not much more. But he was bigger. He was going to be the size of his father and he had the build of a man who worked out with weights - not one of the freaks - one who concentrated on good upper-body development.

"Hello, Andy," I said.

He hadn't expected to see me. I saw him stiffen as if he had learned that the only time any older person spoke to him was when he had done something wrong.

"Let me give you a ride home," I said. "My car's just at the end of the street."

"You don't need to do that. I can take the bus."

"It's no trouble," I said. "I want a word with you, anyway. About Speedy."

He didn't want to talk about Speedy. He didn't want to be quizzed. He was about to refuse to come with me.

"Andy," I said. "Your brother's in serious trouble. There's a chance you can help me to find him."

"I don't know nothin' about Speedy. I don't wanna know."

He was sixteen years old and large for his age, a young bull, trained in obedience and respect but itching to be pushed into a corner and challenged. It wouldn't help matters if he got what he wanted.

"We saw him last night."

"I know all that. They told me this morning."

"Do you know how difficult it can be to start life with a criminal record?"

"I keep my nose clean. What Speedy does is his own business."

"Not your brother's keeper, right?"

For the first time he looked me full in the eye. "That's right."

"Andy, nobody's asking you to look out for Speedy, or hold his hand, or make excuses for anything he does. The thing is, your mother and father care about him, they're eating their hearts out over this. Anything he does that's wrong, they blame themselves for it. He may be headed for big trouble. Think what that would do to your parents."

Maybe it wasn't fair to come at him from that side. He was trying to break free of those ties to family and childhood that kept him dependent, but his family had always been one of the closely knit ones. Anything that could hurt his mother and father he couldn't ignore.

We walked to my car without talking and got in. I didn't start the motor right away.

"Speedy knew where he was going when he walked out on Thursday," I said. "He's part of some sort of group. He knew where he was going and he knew what he was going to do. It's likely that he dropped a hint some time in the past weeks about what he was up to. Can you think of anything that would help me to find him?"

Sullen and troubled, Andy sat next to me staring through the windshield at the row of cars parked in front of us.

"Speedy never talked with me much," he said. "He didn't like me. Used to call me Mr. Gooey Goody. I should have played with him more when he was little."

It wasn't an answer to my question but it showed Andy had started thinking about his relationship with his younger brother. A kid brother can be a pest. A smart quick one can be a thorn in your side. Handled right, though, he might have idolized Andy. Andy would have thrived on that.

"Was Speedy home much when he wasn't at school?" I asked.

"Only for meals."

"Did he talk a lot at the table?"

"Sometimes."

"What about?"

"Anything. Everything. He's a real wise-ass. Give you an argument no matter what you say."

"What's he interested in? Is he serious about anything?"

"Baseball. Got his head full of batting averages and RBI's and records. He likes movies too."

"What about hang-outs? Are there any particular places he favors?"

"I don't know. He never asked me to go with him anywhere. 'Course I never asked him to go anyplace with me. It could be he ran away from me too."

"Andy," I said, "don't start blaming yourself. Things happen. People do things. Maybe if we can find him and get him to come home again..."

"Then maybe I'll know enough to be nicer to him. Even if he is a snotty little shit."

He glanced at me to see my reaction. I laughed. "I think you will," I said.

We drove back to his home and I went in with him. Linda and Jonah were both out so Andy led the way to Speedy's room. It was on the top floor in the front and had a skylight.

There was much of the same excessive neatness about his quarters that I had felt in Leroy's rooms. I had wanted to find a word for what it implied and it came to me now. Both boys were not letting their true natures be seen. There was something secretive about each.

The cot was carefully made. In the small closet, shoes were lined up side by side and clothes hung evenly on hangers. Where Leroy had pictures of ball players thumbtacked to the walls, Speedy had glossy photos of movie actors.

On a desk under the skylight were some of the same school books I'd seen at Leroy's and on a night table by the cot was a stack of Sports Illustrated magazines with the celebrated annual girlie issue on top.

But the room was like a snapshot. It only showed one moment in time. It lacked depth. There were no traces of the toddler or the small boy or the willful volatile child who had lived and grown here. Only a cautious glimpse of an adolescent remained, and it too was a puzzler.

"Didn't Speedy do a lot of reading?" I asked.

Andy nodded. "Yeah. But he started giving away his books a while back, so Momma took the rest and put them in cartons in the cellar."

"What about his interest in baseball? Didn't he have any books of statistics?"

"Didn't need 'em. I told you. He had all that stuff in his head."

The desk and the bureau held nothing of interest. I found myself looking at the only things in the room that anyone would look at - the photos of movie stars.

They were an odd selection. Black actors were poorly represented. A lot of the faces were unknown to me. I recognized Sophia Loren and Danny Kaye and Jack Nicholson. Four pictures seemed to have a place of honor over the bureau. On the left was an early shot of Ingrid Bergman. Then came a face I'd seen but couldn't put a name to. Abbie Hoffman was next and Richard Burton was last. Why had they been given importance?

"Did you get to know any of Speedy's friends?" I asked.

"The last few years he never brought anyone home with him," Andy said. "And he dropped all the little kids he used to go with."

"Wasn't he friends with Leroy Willis?"

"Leroy came here a couple of times. They were real tight, come to think of it."

"Do you know that Leroy has left home too?"

Andy frowned. "That would make sense. So they took off together." He was still scowling. "Something you asked me before - any favorite hang-out. There was one time Leroy came here looking for Speedy and Speedy hadn't come home yet. Leroy said to tell him he'd be down to El Honcho. It was important. I think that was the name. Does that mean anything?"

"Was this recently?"

"Maybe ten days ago. You think..."

El Honcho was a joint on Tremont Street in the South End. I'd never been in it. Didn't know anything about it. Why would two black teen-agers go to a Puerto Rican shop? There was something peculiar about that.

"I don't know what it means, Andy," I said, "but it sounds like the first real lead I've had. I'll check it out."

We went back down the stairs. Linda and Jonah still hadn't come home. Andy came to the door with me.

"Speedy can learn anything faster than anyone else I know," he said. There was admiration and envy, both, in the way he said it. "Maybe he's learning to speak Spanish now."

I thought that was likely to be the only good thing he could learn on that stretch of Tremont Street, but I didn't say so.

"Thank you for talking with me, Andy," I said. I stuck out my hand and he took it. He was young and still awkward in many ways, yet there was much of the assurance of the grown man in him too. His grip was firm but the strength that was there was held back. He was no show-off. He had little of the brilliance his younger brother possessed. He was another one of the pluggers - Costello's word - methodical, steady. He would decide where he was going and nothing would be able to keep him from reaching his destination. Anyone could be proud of a son like that.

15

I spotted a pay phone on Washington Street and parked next to it. It had to have been installed only hours before. No one had wrecked it yet. I dialed and Jerry Frohock answered in the middle of the first ring.

There was no place in the greater Boston area where I could get more information on more people and places and activities than at the downtown office of my old buddy and partner in crime.

"How you doin', Croesus?" I asked.

"Who's that? Jeeter? Is that you?"

"Who else?"

"What's this Croesus bit?"

"Half the money in the world and you don't know who Croesus was. Honestly, Jerry, some of you honkies are sure ignorant."

"Sounds like a Greek. Was he runnin' numbers?"

"Maybe he did. It was kind of a long time ago, though."

"So are you givin' out information, or did you call because you want something?"

"I need something, Jerry. As usual. What do you have on a place on Tremont Street in the South End called El Honcho?"

"Gimme a minute."

Jerry's office is packed with just about every kind of electronic equipment you can think of for storing and compiling information. The stock market, commodities, currency exchanges, bond issues - he's got a rundown on everything happening right up to the last second. Tickers, teletypes, computers, monitors - he sits in the midst of a quarter-million dollars worth of instruments and plays them like some extra terrestrial organist, except that the music he makes is money.

He gets calls from bankers and politicians and managers of funds and big-time gamblers asking his advice. If he puts them onto something that makes them money, they're supposed to send him one per cent of their profits. When there are losses there is no charge. He keeps track of everything. The ones that don't pay get bum steers the next time they call so they quit calling. The ones who benefit pay off in sums that are often staggering. Sometimes the pay-off is in other information. Knowing, one hour sooner than anyone else, that a certain senator is not going to run for re-election, that an adverse medical report is coming in on someone in high office, that a stock split is about to be declared, or that a foreign currency is going to be devalued, can be turned into cash in many ways.

And Jerry likes to keep tabs on what's going on in the city too. Family connections, political and business ties, link-ups with the criminal element, real estate deals - there's very little that escapes his micro-processors.

"You still there, Baby?"

I could almost see the smile on his face. He liked it when I gave him a toughie. I could stick him on ancient history, but never on present-day Boston.

"El Honcho. Variety store occupying street level only. Building belonged to Steven Sullivan et ux until last February. Bought by Peter Rodgers. Peter Rodgers is the new name, legally changed just three years ago, of one Pedro Rodrigues. The sheet on Rodrigues covers car theft, B. & E., armed robbery and sale of controlled substance - a regular little handyman. Is this a friend of yours?"

"I haven't met him yet. Who knows? There are friends and friends. This fellow sounds talented."

"Except this one got caught."

"How much time has he done?"

"Interesting point. None. All suspended sentences."

"So he's probably well-connected."

"That means he's dangerous too. You going after him?"

"I don't know. What I'm looking for is two runaways who maybe used to meet at El Honcho."

"Better wear sneakers and carry a long sharp blade."

"You know I hate knives."

"So strap on the nine millimetre."

"Yes, Mother. Say, how can I make it up to you this time?"

"You know you don't owe me anything, Jeeter. Or go see my Missus and tell her what a great guy I am."

"Will she believe me?"

"No. But it can't do any harm."

"Don't you ever go home anymore, Jerry?"

"Not if I can help it."

"What about your kids?"

"They're all three in college now. Why do you think I need all the money?"

"You worked your way through. Why don't they do the same?"

"They'd just say I was being mean and stingy, so I give them everything they want."

"And that's why they care so much they don't even come see you when they have a vacation."

"Yeah. Well, you can't win 'em all."

"Maybe they'll wise up some day."

"I keep hoping."

"Take care. And thanks."

"You take care, Baby. Where you're going a pair of Dobermans would help."

16

I hung up and got back into the car. I drove down to Blackstone Park and left the Toyota there in front of some old brownstones. Then I walked through West Newton Street to Tremont. With the way everything in that part of town has been increasing in value you'd think Tremont would begin to look better. Instead, it just goes on getting shabbier.

El Honcho was still there. I stood across from it and leaned on a car that looked as if it had been stolen and then abandoned there. It didn't have any plates and two of its tires were flat.

Station #4 was only a few blocks away. It is paradoxical, but the closer you are to a police station the more criminals are likely to be about. And drunks and junkies and bag ladies and panhandlers.

But there were plenty of young people too - the ones who had bought buildings nearby and were fixing them up, and the ones who rented apartments in the fixed-up buildings and worked in insurance companies or offices downtown. Clerks and architects and lawyers, tellers and salesmen and hustlers - you could stand there all day and never get tired of watching all the different types that walked by. Not to mention the young toughs from Castle Square and the Armenians and Orientals and West Indians and gays, the black faces from all over the country and other lands too, and the Spanish-speaking contingent which was growing faster than any of the others.

Most of the faces going in and out of El Honcho were Puerto Rican. Whatever was on sale there, it was an active market. Jerry had called it a variety store. I had the feeling it was a bookie joint. No doubt the cops from the station played their numbers there, if that was the case. The Game is big business now but the Numbers still pay off with a better percentage. Are the so-called criminals who run the numbers game more efficient than the State? Better businessmen? More honest?

I leaned on the car for over two hours, looking up the street as if someone was supposed to be meeting me there, glancing at my watch from time to time, trying to appear impatient and annoyed, meanwhile keeping an eye on the shop.

Nothing unusual happened. Once, a skinny white kid, about twelve years old, went inside and stayed maybe ten minutes before he came out and took off in the direction of the Common. A very slender man wearing a string tie was in and out of the entrance several times. A look out? He eyed me each time he walked out to the street.

Eventually, I took off and went back to my car. There was a ticket under the windshield wiper. I'd need to finagle a resident sticker if I was going to spend much time in that part of town.

I was cold and stiff and hungry so I headed back to the Hill.

A good smell of something roasting met me as I entered my apartment. Flo came out of the kitchen and put her arms around me. She wasn't going to say she'd been worried. She knew it was something she'd have to get used to and live with. On her lips was a taste of apple and nutmeg.

"Applesauce?" I said. "Home made applesauce and a pork roast?"

"I wasn't sure when you'd come back but you timed it just right."

We were still working out ways to fit our two lives together. This was one of the difficult ones. Flo liked cooking, was an excellent cook. But it could only be chance that would bring me home at the right time for something she might prepare. I'd have to remember to phone when I couldn't get back for an evening meal.

And the work she was doing called for adjustments too. For years she had been studying the effects of a complex of contaminents on marine life in a salt marsh. Now, she was putting it all into a paper which would take several months to write. She needed a desk of her own in a room where she could spread out. I would have to let her give my unlisted number to certain marine biologists. I'd have to keep from intruding on those hours when she was concentrating. We were both pretty well set in our habits. There were countless ways in which we could begin to interfere with and irritate each other. I did not want that to happen.

I hung my coat in the closet and washed up. In the kitchen I set the table and got out a bottle of the Beaujolais she liked with her supper. She put the roast on the table along with muffins and leaf spinach and the applesauce and a glass of milk for me.

While we ate, I told her about Ashad and Mrs. Reese and my meeting with Andy and the two hours watching El Honcho.

"Will you go back there?" she asked.

"Tomorrow. If it's open on Sundays. There's a connection there with Speedy and Leroy. I don't know what it is yet. It could be just chance, but it doesn't feel that way."

"This Leroy, he comes from a background completely different from Speedy's. Why would they become friends? Why would both of them run away from home?"

"I think I can see why. They're both black, both fourteen years old, both bused to the same school where most of the other kids are white. They live near each other.

"As for Leroy, he's a kid who's been handed around until he thinks no one cares about him anymore. His own mother just plunked him down with grandma and walked off and hasn't been heard from since. Maybe he never knew his father. Mrs. Reese is a fossil in his eyes and he can't see the kindness and the wisdom in her. It's his age, too. Fourteen is a time of impatience with everything in the adult world, a time of fantasizing and hiding. He was overdue to take off."

"Speedy wasn't."

"How do we know? He may have felt like an outsider too. Andy admitted he hadn't been as nice to his brother as he could have been. Jonah said maybe he'd been too hard on the kid. Linda, over-protective and always wanting to hug him, as if he were a baby, probably irritated him.

"Then along comes this friend. He's fed up with grown-ups, fed up with school. They put their heads together. They find a way to cut loose. They're gone."

"There are others too."

"Right. It's a group. A club. A secret society. They have their own autonomy. Them against the world, perhaps. They could turn into a dangerous gang if they continue to do things that are crooked."

"Then where does the variety store fit in?"

"I don't know. Leroy left word with Andy that Speedy should meet him there once. It's not the kind of place where teen-agers would be likely to hang out. I'm almost certain it's a bookie joint. That could make it a message center, too. And the man who owns the building is a known criminal. If any of this can lead me to Speedy, I've got to pursue it."

We shared an orange for dessert and then I did the cleaning up.

Flo had emptied all my cabinets one day and had washed every corner of them and put in new shelf paper. She'd made changes in where I kept things. That had bothered me. But my first feeling of annoyance had quickly given way to acceptance of the fact that the changes were logical, and of course she had every right to arrange things for her own convenience too.

She was adjusting to living in close quarters with a new man after a decade with Tom Porter in their home on the Cape where she'd had a whole suite of her own. It was not a simple transition for her. She was thirty-eight years old now. There was a lot she had given up when she moved in with me. Would she come to regret the amenities she'd once had, the greater freedom, the tidal plain and salt marsh which had been at her doorstep for so many years?

"I wonder if one of the boys I saw at the Centrum was Leroy?" she asked. "I'm almost sure there were four who were selling phony tickets and two of the them were black. They were a long way off and I only saw them for a couple of seconds, but I might be able to identify Leroy if I saw him again - or if I had a photo of him."

I put the last dish in the rack to dry and started sponging off the counters.

"Maybe some afternoon I could visit Linda," she said. "We could go together to see Mrs. Reese and ask if she has a photo."

It was something she wanted to do. I could tell. With Linda, she had quickly been at ease. Not so with Jonah. She had never been around black people before she met me and she knew that if we were to stay together we would often be in mixed company. It was important to her to understand the reticence and the mistrust which would be a black response to her, just the way all of us have had to learn to deal with the supicion and withdrawal so many white people feel for blacks. She needed to test her own feelings too. I know what it's like to step into a room full of white people who are strangers. I've done it many times. Flo was going to have to find out what it's like to step into a room full of black people. Prejudice is a two-way street.

"Phone her any time you want," I said. "The number's in the smaller book next to the directory. You and Linda might get to be friends."

"Would that complicate matters?"

"I don't think so."

"She's very lovely."

"So are you."

"You and she were lovers once. That's not a thing you forget."

"You and I are lovers now. That's not a thing I would put in jeopardy."

I'd thought a lot about our relationship, asked myself some difficult questions. How much of what drew us together had to do with a natural attraction of opposites or forbidden fruit? That was one of the tough ones. I admitted it added to the excitement. But had that been all that we shared it wouldn't have been enough to hold us together more than a moment. I've slept with other white women. I was curious. So were they. Plenty of white women get the idea they'd like to check out a black stud. Why not? But that's only another form of promiscuity. Nothing enduring comes of it.

How about the fact that Flo had saved my life, not too many months ago? I had to be grateful to her, didn't I? But that's a faulty base on which to build. None of us likes to be beholding. It's human nature to resent all favors that aren't earned.

Sometimes I've looked around at other couples, some married, some not. Aside from mammoth portions of self-deception and the unquestioned power of intense physical attraction, what makes most unions strongest is genuine admiration, on both sides, for the capabilities and qualities of their partner. Was that what we had, Flo and I? I wanted to think so.

17

For three days I watched El Honcho. I didn't try to stay hidden. Two of the days I double-parked across the street and simply sat in my Toyota. It was more comfortable that way.

One noon, half a dozen expensive limousines drew up in front of the shop. The drivers stayed in the cars with the motors running while an assortment of mostly heavy-set, conservatively-dressed types went into the shop for fifteen minutes before coming out again and driving away. Not long after they left, a cruiser stopped out front. One of the two cops in it got out. He was a sergeant, close to retirement age. He went inside and reappeared two minutes later with a small brown paper bag and a sack of potato chips in his left hand. He was munching the potato chips as he got back into the cruiser.

The regular patrons of the shop were people from the neighborhood - working people, people on Social Security, people on disability or welfare, unless I missed my guess. Occasionally someone would come out of the place with a bottle of Pepsi or a milk carton. Most, simply went in, put their quarter or whatever on a number, and came back out. As far as I could tell, nobody made a hit while I was watching. Or if anyone did go in to collect he, or she, must have done it as unobtrusively as possible. There is no percentage in advertising that you have a roll of bills on you if you're walking around alone in the city.

Only twice did I see some youngster who looked out of place go into the shop. Each, like the white kid from Saturday afternoon, was only inside a short time, then came out and took off in the direction of the Common.

It was late Tuesday when I spotted the second one. He was thin and long. He had that kind of bouncy walk you see sometimes when an individual goes up on his toes as his weight comes forward for the next step.

I got out of the car and followed him, keeping to the other side of the street. It was after dark but he was easy to see because he had on a light cap that bobbed up and down like the ball they used to put on the movie screen when there was a sing-along. He had no idea I was trailing him.

When he crossed Boylston Street, he headed up the long diagonal path across the Common. There were very few people around then. I made sure no one was following me and went after the Bouncer.

He was about a hundred yards ahead of me as he got to Beacon Street. A car stopped where he was stepping off the sidewalk. It cut off my view of him. As I approached it, three men got out and came toward me. One was the look-out, the man from the shop who always wore a string tie. They'd known where the kid was going, had driven right to the spot and blocked me from any further pursuit. I saw the light cap bob a couple more times and then disappear.

The three men fanned out to form a triangle, each about fifteen feet away. The look-out stood in front of me, his hands crossed over his skinny chest but something in his right hand under his left armpit, probably a switch blade. No doubt the others had a blade ready too. Jerry had been right.

"Now you gonna tal us wat you doin', Man." It was the guy in front of me who had spoken.

"Just strolling through the park," I said.

"You fahnny, Man."

Each moved a bit closer to me. Cars were passing, fifty yards ahead. There was no one behind me in the Common, but the three would have to hurry or someone would be along and that would provide a witness. Maybe.

"You gonna tal me wat you doin'?"

They were closer on all three sides now, but no one had snapped a blade open yet. Too bad I'd left my gun at home.

"Sure," I said. "I'll tell you anything you want to know."

While I said it I stepped toward the man in front of me. As expected, his right hand came forward and a blade snicked out pointed at my guts, but I had already aimed a kick at his arm. The toe of my shoe caught the big outside bone in his wrist. Something cracked. His knife flew away into the darkness. I was on him then and grabbed his good arm and spun him. He was so light I could have picked him up and thrown him against a tree. Instead, I used his body as a shield and met the closer man who was charging in. His blade knicked his boss in the cheek as he tried to draw away and he fell over backwards when I shoved him. I stomped the hand in which he held his knife and turned to face the third man. He'd gone. He was high-tailing it for the car which burned rubber a moment later and disappeared into traffic.

I dropped the skinny one on his buddy's legs and then picked up the blade that was close to my feet. It was a beauty. I tested the edge on the back of a thumbnail. It couldn't have been any sharper.

"Don't try to stand up," I told the two men on the ground. I wiped the knife on the shirt of the man on top, then slipped the blade back into the handle and pocketed it.

"Your turn to talk now," I said, but before I finished saying it I knew that they weren't going to talk. Blood was flowing from the cut on one's check and the broken wrist must have been very painful. As for the hand I'd stomped, there were small broken bones there too and they would be hurting, but neither man let any feelings show. They were small-time flunkies and not even very good at what they should have known best, but a code of silence was one thing they had learned. Short of torture, they were not going to say a word.

A man with a briefcase came along the path. He took in the scene without breaking stride. Maybe he'd look for a phone and report a black man standing over two other men, one obviously injured. More than likely, he wouldn't. But someone would be coming for these two guys soon. They wouldn't come alone. I had to get moving. Was there any point in saying anything to the two crummies on the ground? Probably not. I turned my back on them, walked to Beacon Street and flagged a cab.

When we pulled up next to my car, two kids wearing coveralls had just reached it. One stood ready to lift the hood and the other was slipping a piece of spring steel into the opening between the driver's door and the frame. I gave the cabbie a five and jumped out.

"Beat it," I said.

The one trying to get the door open stepped back. Up close, I saw he wasn't so young after all. Neither was his partner. Passers-by had heard me. There'd be an army on me if I didn't move quickly. The man in front of me put his hand behind him as if to draw a knife. He still had the sharp piece of spring steel in his other hand.

The door to the cab slammed and we all glanced that way. A couple of cars braked to a stop behind the cab. People were moving in on all sides.

The cab driver had a tire iron in his meaty fist. He raised his arm and took a step toward the second thief.

The guy in front of me went into the air like a grasshopper and came down running. His pal followed him. Several figures were beginning to converge on me.

"Time to go," I said to the cabbie. "And thanks."

The cab shot off up Tremont. I pulled out after him, wheels spinning, and headed back to the Hill.

18

They knew too much about me now. I'd thought I could get them out in the open by showing myself, but I hadn't learned anything and instead they knew my car, my license plate, my face and, if they had any connection at the Registry, they could even have my name. The only address they could have obtained was a PO box number and that was a bank slot that I rarely used. The friend who managed my building when I wasn't living in it, and who worked in the bank, let me know when anything came for me at that address. If they had a way to stake out the Post Office they could wait there a year and never get any closer to where I lived.

My car, though, was not going to be much use around town anymore, so the next morning I put it in a garage in Watertown and got a somewhat battered, but still serviceable, Ford from Rent-a-wreck. Back in business.

But where to start? Were the kids I'd seen go in and out of El Honcho connected with Speedy and Leroy? If they weren't, I'd already wasted a lot of time. I was sure I'd recognize them if I saw them again. Were they crashing on the Hill someplace, or nearby? It had been late afternoon when each one appeared. I could haunt the Beacon Street side of the Hill at dusk each day and hope to spot one of them, but that seemed like a million-to-one shot. Better scratch it.

I could go after Pedro Rodrigues. There had to be a way to find him. Maybe to lean on him. To squeeze something out of him. But I had no assurance that he had anything to do with runaway kids. Maybe he was just a numbers operator. Besides, the folks down at El Honcho wouldn't be feeling any special affection for me now.

I decided to go back to the school.

There was a parking place for the principal. Three other places had names on them. Teachers? The one marked Mr. O'Connor was empty so I slid the Ford in there.

Seated on a cement parapet were four kids who looked to be the right age to be students. All four were white, male, and decked out like bikies - black boots, jeans, leather jackets. Dress codes went out a long time ago. This quartet had settled for a uniform. They were passing a cigarette from one to the other. A joint.

They watched me get out of the car and approach them, defiance in their look. They were minors and had immunity and nothing fazed them. If they wanted to cut classes and smoke pot, so what? "Go on, suspend me," their look said, "then I won't even have to go to school." Maybe they'd already been suspended.

"I'm looking for two students who seem to have dropped out," I said.

There was no reaction from any of the four.

Names are Eric Johnson and Leroy Willis."

Still no response.

"Do you know them?"

The boy who was trying to suck one more drag out of the cigarette inhaled, then held it a second before flicking the butt onto the black top. When he had exhaled he said, "We don't know nothin'."

"Yeah," said the one on his left, "they learned us that in school - we don't know nothin'." They all sniggered.

I let a sort of smile appear around my mouth. Then I asked, "What class are you in?"

"Lower class," he said. A wit.

"I mean what class in school?"

"Third year freshman." Now they were all laughing.

"So you must know Speedy."

"You some kinda truant officer?"

"No."

"Cop?"

"Nope."

"Why you lookin' for Speedy and Willis?"

"They're in trouble."

"What kinda trouble?"

"Don't you know?"

"I awready tole you - we don't know nothin'."

"I think every one of you knows a lot of things," I said. "Speedy and Leroy may not be the only ones in trouble from this school. They're wanted for grand larceny, fraud, forgery - who knows what all the charges will be? I'm not trying to catch them to turn them in. I want to get them out of trouble before they get in over their heads. What can you guys tell me?"

For a moment I think they had been ready to talk. They'd relaxed and had a laugh. A door had come part way open. Now it slammed shut again. I'd reached for the handle and they didn't allow that.

One of them spat toward my shoes and then crossed his arms over his chest. Each one of the others, in turn, did the same. They sat there in a line on that cold cement and stared at me out of eyes already lifeless, little old dead men in a cannabis trance. They'd finished talking.

"All right," I said. "I just hope you'll all still be here when I come back out."

I turned and went into the school building. The principal's office was down a corridor to the left on the main floor. Two girls were slouched on a bench outside. One was crying and snuffling. A muscle-bound matron sat at a desk behind a pile of forms. She took one at a time, looked at a list in front of her, made a check on it and set the form in a second pile on the opposite corner of her desk.

The administrative make-work machine. Get a thousand students to fill out a thousand forms. Check the thousand forms against a thousand lists. File the thousand forms in a thousand files. A committee finds the forms faulty. Start over.

"Excuse me," I said.

The lady did not look up.

"Excuse me," I said again. "I would like to see the principal."

"He's busy." Nothing I could say was going to make her break her rhythm.

I put my hand on the top of the pile from which she was ready to take another form. Her hand touched mine and she recoiled.

"It troubles me," I said, "to interrupt work as stimulating and creative as yours, but if the chief is in, I want to see him."

Had she thought I was another student sent down to see the principal? Was she going to wipe her hand on her skirt to get rid of the contamination? Just for the record, her skirt looked as if she'd wiped her hands on it quite a few times already.

"If you don't have an appointment," she said, "you'll have to come back another day."

"I might come back another day, too," I said, "but right now I'm going to see the big man even without an appointment. It will only take a couple of minutes. If he's busy handing out demerits, he can give me one too, before these young ladies on the bench get theirs. You won't mind, will you?" I asked, turning to them.

The one who had been crying blinked away her tears.

"You can take my place anytime," she said.

"Be my guest," said the other one.

I gave the doll at the desk my most winning smile. "You see," I said. "No trouble at all."

The door behind her opened. A third girl came out. She made a face and mouthed the word 'bastard' as she started down the corridor.

Before the matron could get out of her chair, I stepped into the principal's office and closed the door behind me. The man before me was busy filling out forms. They are really overworked these days. By the time they get through with attendance lists and rules of conduct and records on discipline and what marks everyone gets in every class and who is in Special Needs, it's a wonder if there's time to open a book.

The principal was in his late fifties. He wore thick glasses and had a triple chin. A copy of the Declaration of Independence hung on the wall behind him. I couldn't help thinking how inappropriate its sentiments were in an institution such as this.

He finished putting checks in boxes on the form and looked up. Did a double take.

"You're not a student here," he said. "I'm seeing students this period."

"Variety is the spice of life," I said.

He didn't think that was funny. It was obvious that he had been 'integrated' right up to his limit, and he never had liked Negroes anyway.

"Who are you? And what is your business here?"

"I'm investigating the disappearance of two of your students."

"Are you a police officer?"

"Private investigator."

"Credentials?"

I handed him my ticket. He got out a lined file card and took pains to write down name, age, height...he would have xeroxed it if he'd had a copier at hand. Maybe he was preparing to file a complaint. Good.

"Now what do you think I can do for you?"

"Eric Johnson," I said. "Nicknamed Speedy. And Leroy Willis. Both freshmen this year. Both black. Can you tell me anything about them?

"Surely you don't expect me to know every student by name."

"Perhaps these two got sent to you for disciplining enough times so you'd remember them."

"The black students who've been bused to this school have consistently been trouble-makers. However, I find it difficult to distinguish one from another."

"You mean if I showed you a photograph of Alice Walker and one of James Baldwin and one of Martin Luther King, you couldn't tell them apart. Is that right?"

He probably didn't even know who the first two were.

"I'm afraid I don't see where this conversation is getting us," he said.

"What happens when a student stops coming to school?"

"We send someone to find him, or her."

"Are records kept of drop-outs?"

"We keep very careful records on all our students."

Yeah. That could have been how he got the job. He wasn't an educator. He was an accountant. Or some politician's brother-in-law.

"Who is the person you send after drop-outs?"

"It varies."

"Who's working on it today?"

"I have no idea."

"Where are the records on drop-outs?"

"Those are not open to anyone who just happens to pop in." He was beginning to enjoy himself. "You'd need a letter from the Superintendant in order to have access to them." Now he was actually smiling - a wan constipated smile.

Had he ever had children of his own? Had he ever been a child himself? He was the kind of prissy little martinet who had probably never enjoyed anything as much as playing games like Giant Steps and sending other players back to start over again.

"Tell you what, Prince," I said. "I'll make a deal with you."

The smile vanished. "I do not make deals," he said.

"You might make this one, though. You tell me where I can meet this truant officer of yours and for at least five minutes I will refrain from stuffing your face into the nearest toilet."

He started to stand up, but before he could get all the way to his feet I was around his desk and nose to nose with him. "Where?" I repeated. "Your five minutes are going fast."

He wanted to retreat, but his chair was against the back of his knees. He sank into it again.

"He's in room B-3 right now," he said.

"You're certain? I wouldn't want to have to disturb you again."

"I'm certain."

"Thank you," I said. "My report will state that you gave wholehearted support to the investigation."

What report? To whom? Maybe that would keep him quiet for a few minutes. He wasn't much of a battler. Handing out demerits to little girls was about all he was good for.

19

The B stood for Basement and number 3 was a windowless cubicle, more a closet than a room.

A short man, about my own age, wearing a rumpled brown suit, and chewing gum, sat at a makeshift desk. He was preparing a list of addresses. His day's work. The list was a long one.

"Sorry to bother you," I said, "but I could use some help."

"So could I. What do you want?"

I asked him if he had Johnson and Willis on his list. He looked. "Sure do. You know them?"

"They seem to be runaways. I know Speedy Johnson and his family. Leroy, I've never met but I've talked with his grandmother, Mrs. Reese."

"You can save me two stops if you have answers to a few questions."

I gave him what he needed and he was genuinely grateful.

"Do you have a list of drop-outs?" I asked.

"Yup. You want to see it?"

I said I would.

He hauled a carton from under his desk and found a folder in it which he handed to me. Tut tut. The Superintendant wasn't going to like this.

"Those are the ones since school started this fall," he said. "You want the ones from previous years?"

I said that wouldn't be necessary, but how about recent unexcused absences?

"That's what I'm working on now," he said. "Most of these are kids who'll be back. A nudge from us, a whack from a guardian or parent, and they reappear. For a while. A couple we won't be able to locate. Maybe they landed a job. Maybe they moved away. Sometimes the whole family is gone. Got in debt and skipped."

"You don't get to know any of these youngsters, do you?"

"Hardly ever see anyone twice. A lot I never even see once. There something special about the two you're after?"

"They've gone into crime."

"That's not so special."

"These two were part of a scam that cleared them over four thousand dollars. And it was organized."

"Some other kids from here might have been in on it too. Is that it?"

"Right. It looks like a group of juveniles. Speedy is an exceptionally bright boy. Maybe the others are too. If I can get to them soon enough, there may be something to salvage."

"You want copies of these two lists?"

"I'd appreciate it."

He went into the hall. Must have crossed over to the Graphics room. He was back in barely a minute.

"Thanks," I said. "They call me Jeeter."

"Jeeter," he repeated. "Now there's a moniker to hang onto. They always called me Dunk. Never could shake loose of it. Good luck. And come again if I can help in any way."

I walked back upstairs thinking how the decent people - like Costello and Dunk - wound up in the cellar and the turds all floated to the top. Well, maybe it wasn't always that way.

The cold outside air was a relief after the over-heated, stuffy air of the school, but when I neared my car I found that all four tires were flat and the same quartet of potheads was still perched on the cement wall. They'd been waiting quite a while. Didn't want to miss the fun. It wouldn't be fair to disappoint them.

I pretended I didn't see them. Opened the trunk of the car. When I rented the car, the agent told me that one of the tires had a slow leak and there was a pump in back, just in case. It was there. An old-fashioned bicycle pump. Perfect.

I walked over to the group. Those dead-pan, half-dead faces didn't waver. Only the eyeballs swiveled under reptilian lids to follow my approach.

"You," I said, and I poked a finger into the chest of the one who had spoken with me before. "Take off your jacket."

The three others pushed off from the wall and were standing.

"Get back where you were," I said. "Before you annoy me."

The one nearest me went to push my shoulder. I ducked under his shove, put a gentle jab into his solar plexis and gave his left cheek a resounding open-handed smack. He crumpled. The two others got back on the parapet.

"Take off the jacket," I said again.

"Man, it's cold out here. You crazy?" His teeth were chattering just from sitting there waiting for me. Now he was scared too.

"In less than five minutes you'll be sweating," I said. "Now take it off, or I'll rip it off for you."

He got down from the wall and slowly removed the jacket. Only a tank top was underneath it and it was dirty and torn. I took the jacket out of his hands and said, "Follow me."

He came along reluctantly as I went back to the car.

"Get the pump out of the trunk."

He was turning blue and his hands were shaking, but he lifted the pump out while I put his jacket inside and slammed down the lid.

"Just so you don't get any ideas about running away," I said. "Now put air back into the tires."

"With this?" he wailed. He was almost crying. "It'll take all day."

"But it'll warm you up so you won't die of pneumonia, won't it?"

There were actually tears in his eyes. He looked at his buddies. No support there.

He hooked up the pump and started work. An hour and ten minutes later, bushed, soaked with sweat, hands blistered, he was through. There was enough air in the four tires to get me to a service station. I put the pump back in the trunk and helped him on with his jacket.

"A work-out like that once a day," I told him, "and you could make the team. Go home and take a hot shower. You're going to have a lot of strange new stiff muscles tomorrow. But you're all right." I couldn't keep a half smile off my face. I might have caved in myself if I'd had to do what he'd just done.

20

"She took me downstairs to their kitchen," Flo said. "She'd just put a sweet potato pie in the oven. When she got things cleaned up, she sat with me at the big table there.

"For a while we were both rather uncomfortable, not really knowing how to behave, being too formal and then trying too hard to be casual. Suddenly, both of us realized it and we started laughing. From then on it was as if we had known each other for years and only had to catch up on what had happened since we'd last seen each other."

It was almost midnight. Flo and I were in bed. The lamp on the table on my side was lit. Flo sat cross-legged, elbows on knees, spectacularly naked, facing me where I was propped against the pillows. I wanted to hear about this meeting, but it was not easy to concentrate on it alone.

"She's frantic with worry about Speedy. Keeps imagining awful things that could happen to him. Blames herself. Wonders what she should have done that she didn't.

"Jonah was working and Andy was at school. She's alone almost all day during the week. Jonah works Saturdays, too, so that Sunday is about the only day she has someone to talk to. I don't think she has other close friends.

"Her whole life is her family and home - wife, mother and homemaker. The unliberated woman. Every man's dream."

"Times have changed," I said.

"And Linda's dream has turned into a nightmare. What went wrong? Should she have been less compliant with Jonah, or did she not give in enough? She's asking herself lots of questions about him. She's totally devoted to him, but she's watched both her boys grow into young men and leave her and Jonah behind - leave them out. The world has changed, not just the times, and she and Jonah haven't moved with it but their children have. 'Maybe it's what always happens,' she said. She was thinking about how she had grown away from her parents, I believe.

"She talked about you, too. She was precise and lucid about how it couldn't have worked out for the two of you. She knew what she wanted and she saw that one or the other of you would have had to give up something essential in order to stay together and that would have undermined what you did have. She can be frighteningly clear-headed."

"And then Jonah came along."

"Yes. Jonah. She called him a big soft-hearted lion. She knew he was what she needed. She knows, too, how much she hurt you. She's profoundly aware of what others feel, and she has something that is rare in this I'll-get-mine-first world - it's not simply that she will give unstintingly of herself to those she loves. She has true generosity."

Flo was generous too. I'd never thought about it before, but this was a common element in the women who have been important to me. With Flo, though, there was a mind moving side by side with natural impulse, analyzing effectiveness, losses and gains. With Linda the impulse came first, appraisal later.

"When the pie was done, I told her how I wanted to visit Mrs. Reese to see if she had a photo of Leroy. Linda had never called on her before, though she knew where she lived. We put on coats and Linda took a plant from the window sill in the kitchen and brought it along.

"We sat in the front room. Mrs. Reese has a chair by the window from which she can see what goes on in the street. Whenever a person or a car passed, she would look that way. There was a feeling of constraint in the room. I think Linda does not see many other people and is a little shy. There was the big difference in age between her and Mrs. Reese. Then there was my presence and neither of them could be sure what I was thinking. Or feeling.

"Linda took the plant out of the paper bag she had brought it in and gave it to Mrs. Reese. That old lady held it in her cupped hands as if it were something fragile and precious. 'A rose geranium,' she said. Maybe it reminded her of some other time or place, or maybe it had simply been years since anyone had thought to bring her a present, however simple. Her old wrinkled face altered. Her eyes narrowed. She was looking inward and smiling, a child again with a secret source of pleasure, a private joy.

"It made all the difference. You see? Linda has a spontaneous, uncalculated instinct for giving. It could be a word or a gesture, sometimes an object. Even without any of these, you sense it in her - a warmth that is innate and without design. She's a beautiful person."

"I know."

Flo's eyes were on mine, trying to see or determine how much Linda still meant to me. Did I know myself? Almost nineteen years had passed since we met. I was twenty-two. She had just had her seventeenth birthday. She moved in with me in the back room I had in a rooming house on St. Botolph Street. There was no moment when I wasn't working that we didn't spend together. In forty-one years I have never loved any other woman the way I loved Linda.

"Would you go back to her," Flo asked, "if something happened to Jonah?"

"No."

"Even if I were not here?"

"Probably not."

"Why?"

"Have you ever gone back to a place where you once lived?" I asked. "Have you ever gone looking for something you had and you lost? You never find it, you know. Parts of it maybe. Fragments. You can reawaken memory, stir up old ghosts of yourself and of others. If it's just out of curiosity, if it doesn't matter, there's not much harm in it. But love is something else. There is a time to love. Once you've had it you should not turn back."

"Is that a way of finding an excuse for breaking new ground?"

"Male chauvinism, you mean. But I'm not talking about dropping one partner for another. I'm talking about trying to recapture something lost a long time ago. It can only lead to disappointment."

"But you still love her."

"I still care about her. We shared something important once. I don't understand throwing away old friendships or former lovers, the way you toss out an old shirt, just because lives have run in different directions. Do you?"

She didn't answer. Perhaps she was thinking about her husband, on whom she had turned her back. There could be justification for that. It was foolish to make generalizations. Every relationship is different.

In the yellow incandescent light her skin was the color of old ivory. I wanted to reach for her and draw her against me, but she hadn't finished yet.

"When I asked if she had a photo of Leroy, Mrs. Reese went into the back room that was her bedroom, I think, and returned with a school picture. She said it was the only one she had. All the members of the eighth grade were in it, in bright color, and Leroy stood at the left end of the front row with his arms crossed. There was a stubborn rebellious look on his face. He wasn't smiling, the way so many others were. He was dressed differently, but I'm almost certain he is the same boy I saw in Worcester.

"I told her so. She didn't seem to be upset. I had the feeling she'd already been through this sort of thing and knew the outcome and accepted it. She was like a bridge across a river which would not be swept away."

I put my hand on Flo's knee, smooth and cool, and my eyes traveled up her leg to the shadowed roseate lips that had enclosed me so many times already. She saw me looking. She drew the sheet back from where it coverd me and let her fingers trail up my thighs and dance on me.

She too was a bridge, a bridge into a world of mutual caring and sustenance if we were to stay together. We had looked at the obstacles and talked about them. For the moment they were as unimportant as fly specks on a window.

21

Speedy had been gone for five days. Time enough to begin to miss his mother's good cooking, a bed of his own in his own room, the trust and love (whether he valued them or not) of his mother and father. Wouldn't he be feeling homesick by now, I wondered?

Or was there enough excitement in being on his own and in doing something dangerous to compensate for things that had become dull, even oppressive?

I tried to remember what it was like to be fourteen, but my mind filled with stereotypical words and images that got in the way. Certainly I'd been almost totally wrapped up in myself. At that age it's a rare individual who asks what anyone else is feeling. Even Speedy, smarter than most, maybe because of that, would not be thinking about the pain and anxiety he could cause.

Or would he? By now he would have started making comparisons. Had he been hungry or cold yet? Was it easy sleeping in surroundings that were noisy or dirty, without a pillow perhaps, or one that was soiled? Where did he go to the bathroom? If Leroy was not his only companion, who were the others and how did he adjust to their different ways? It's too easy to take good things for granted. He'd have found that out by now, wouldn't he?

Somehow I had to find him before he got set in a way of life which could make normal existence impossible - before he fell ill, before he became drug-addicted, before criminal activity became habitual. Surely there was still time. But where was he?

Once more I went to see Ashad, this time taking the dropout list and the one of recent unexcused absences with me. In less than twenty minutes we came up with another runaway from the school. His name was Timothy Burgess. He'd dropped out at the end of September. The address was on Mass Ave near the corner of Columbus Avenue in the South End. Ashad had a photo of Timothy. He was the white kid I'd seen running away before he got tackled in Worcester.

The woman who opened the door had enough flesh on her to make two of me. A shapeless cotton dress hung on her like a sheet over a piece of furniture. Her arms were bare. They were the arms of a bouncer in an after-hours club.

"I'm looking for Timothy Burgess," I said. "Is he here?"

"He ain't to home."

"Can you tell me where he is?"

"Nope."

"You're not his mother, are you."

"Not yours either. Whaddaya want?"

"Timothy seems to be a runaway and he's in trouble." I made a guess. "Is he a ward of yours?"

"You ain't told me who you are or what you're after."

I decided to go along with her. "I'm a private investigator," I said. "Two other kids from the school Timothy attended have taken off with him. At least it looks as if they're all together. The parents of Speedy Johnson have asked me to help find their son. Leroy Willis is the third boy. I'm not working for the police. I only want to find Speedy and try to make him return home before all of these youngsters get caught and sent away. I'm sure you'd like to have Timothy back for the same reason."

I was betting that her only interest in Timothy was the check she got for his maintenance. She probably had him out working part-time jobs too and took a big share of whatever he earned that way. If she got him back and he was in crime, she might have even more to gain.

There are too many well-nigh sexless fiftyish females in the business of taking on foster kids in the city. The State tries to find homes for them. The stubborn ones, the hard cases, wind up with people like the one before me. The only milk of human kindness in her was colored green, and if you squeezed her for a week you wouldn't get enough of it to fill an eye dropper.

"Have you any idea where Timothy might have gone?" I asked.

She hated to give anything away, and she had something. What's more, if I got Timothy back she'd be on the payroll again. He'd been out of school and gone for two months almost certainly, but she'd only reported him missing one week ago which would have stopped her check for his care.

I took a twenty from my billfold but kept a tight grip on one end of it. She put her hand out, palm up.

"Look for a wino named O'Leary in the taverns along Cambridge Street in the West End," she said. "Tim used to go to his place with some other kids. You find O'Leary and you'll find Tim."

I'm sure she knew that if it was a bum steer I'd be back, but maybe she wasn't afraid of me. She didn't look like a type that had ever been intimidated by anyone. I gave her the twenty. It turned out to be money well spent.

22

Two hours later, in the third cafe I entered, the owner said sure he knew O'Leary, and he told me how to find where he lived. It was on Hancock Street.

I'd left the rental car parked in the MGH garage and was on foot. O'Leary's place was just around the corner, not all that far from my own building on Revere Street.

I rang every bell in the place and couldn't get an answer so I started knocking on the front door. Probably all the tenants worked. Maybe most of the bells didn't. But there had to be someone around. When I was almost ready to give up, a bleary-eyed man of indeterminate age opened the door.

"No need to be batterin' the house down," he said. "What do you want?"

"Are you Mr. O'Leary?" I asked.

"Himself," he said, and made an attempt to square his shoulders and look me in the eye. But he was a sad weak travesty of a man, down at the heel, malnourished, sickly.

"I'd appreciate a chance to talk with you," I said.

"And what about? I have work to do."

I didn't ask him what the work was. I could well imagine.

"It's about a young boy named Timothy Burgess."

His eyes narrowed and I realized I'd made it sound as if there might be a morals charge involved. Maybe there was. I kept silent, studying his reaction.

Standing in the open door, he began to shiver. It wasn't very cold out, but the wind was off the ocean and it was raw.

"I don't suppose you'd just go away, if I asked you to," he said.

I shook my head.

"Then you might as well come in."

I stepped into the hallway. He shut the door behind me. "This way," he said. "My quarters lack something of elegance, but what they lack in style they make up for in warmth."

He led the way downstairs to the basement. He had a sort of room next to an old steam boiler with a tankless hot water heater on one side, risers off the center with four-inch flanges just below the ceiling, asbestos insulation over all the pipes.

Warm, it surely was. I started sweating immediately. O'Leary, instead, was in his element. And he had a jug on a makeshift table by the cot where he slept. He downed a glass of red wine, let me have the only chair, and sat on the edge of his unmade bed. He offered me none of the wine.

"I'm in charge of maintenance here," he said, without being asked. "In return, I get a place to live, such as it is. We've seen better days."

Was that an imperial 'we', or was he not alone? It didn't seem likely that anyone else could share such cramped confines.

"Now what would you be after wantin' to know about Timothy Burgess?"

"Have you seen him recently?"

"Maybe I have and maybe I haven't. Is it that gross strumpet across town wants to know?"

"Do you know her?"

"A vicious, heartless woman she is. She'd sell her own soul if there were a way to do it. Poor little Timmy could not have fallen into greedier hands."

"How did you come to know them?"

"I have friends in the South End. Some very influential people, I'll have you know. I visit them now and then. 'Course the times they are a-changin'. What goes up must come down, so they say. I met Timmy ridin' on the bus one day. We sat side by side, got talkin', struck up a friendship. He told me about the old bat had him in her care and I went to see if what he said was true about how mean she was and how she treated him. I barely got inside before she assisted my departure."

"You mean she threw you out."

"Arse over teakettle, as the sayin' goes. That one could get in the ring with Killer Casey and he'd run home cryin'."

"So then Timothy started coming to see you here."

O'Leary didn't answer right away. He filled his glass again and drank half of it. He'd been drinking since early morning, no doubt. Did he ever eat anything? There was no sign of food in this cave where he lived. I'd noticed a toilet just outside the boiler room door, but no place where he could wash up or draw water.

He had stacked newspapers against the wall behind his cot and around it so that he literally had a hole he could crawl into. He had brought Timothy here, other young boys too perhaps - a gift of gab, a look of being harmless, pretended or maybe even genuine sympathy. Classic. And an alcoholic, of course.

He knew I'd put it together. He had all the cunning of a city rat. How many times had he been beaten yet still survived? He watched me and I was sure he understood I wouldn't hurt him, no matter what my personal feelings might be.

"Sure, Timmy has stayed here sometimes," he said. "He's an orphan, you know. Never knew either of his parents. I'm his friend and he knows it."

"Where is he now?" I asked.

"I don't know."

"How long since you've seen him?"

"More than a week."

"Do you know that last Friday night he and three other boys got away with over four thousand dollars?"

O'Leary's eyebrows went up. Then he turned his head to one side. "And they haven't been caught?"

"No. But it's only a matter of time."

He pondered that for a moment. "Was it a hold-up?"

He really didn't know, so I told him.

"Clever," he said. "And organized. Timmy said once there was an organization."

He finished the wine in his glass and refilled it. What he'd had so far was beginning to affect him. How much did he get through every day? The bottle on the table held one point seven five liters - less than half a gallon. Empties filled the space under his cot. Drunks hate to throw out evidence of their 'work,' the only tangible proof of what they do with their lives.

"Where's Timothy been living?" I asked.

"I don't know."

"Do you think it's in the city?"

"I think it's nearby. Right here on the Hill someplace. But I don't know where."

"He's not alone, is he?"

"I have no way of bein' certain, but I don't think so. He used to talk with me about what he was doin' and what he hoped to make of himself, but lately he's become very secretive. He was driftin' away from me, had found other companions, I guess.

"I told him to set his sights high. I said don't look at me. It put me in mind of a sermon I once heard. 'No man is worthless,' the preacher told us. 'He can always serve as a bad example.' But the young are not given to heedin' the lessons of their elders."

A couple more hours of drinking and this derelict would be quoting JM Singe or spouting poetry. He had a silken tongue. Had not always put it to noble purpose.

"How did Timothy get in touch with you?" I asked.

"He'd come through the alley and tap on the window by the back door where I keep the trash barrels."

"Was there any predictable day, or time of day, he'd come?"

"No. It wouldn't seem so. You know, if you manage to find him, I wouldn't want him to think I'd been the one to betray him. You won't tell him you've spoken with me, will you?"

"There's no reason to do so."

He cleared his throat. "Would you have a fiver you could give to an old man?"

I'd felt it coming. He'd given me next to nothing, but he wanted something for it all the same. I knew what he'd do with the money.

"What do you live on?" I asked. "Are you on Welfare?"

"I'm on Disability."

Of course. They didn't call it Welfare. Being disabled was almost like being a veteran. They owed you something. And drink was surely disabling. The only trouble was that with a check twice a month a drunk could stay drunk just about as long as he lived. And the thing about that was that the cheap booze was a short road to an early death.

I gave him the five, knowing I was just helping him on his way.

23

Somewhere in my subconscious I must have registered the fact that a car was double-parked up the street when I left O'Leary. It was just after dark. I was half way to the corner when I heard a squeal of rubber and sensed that someone was after me. Without even looking, I dropped to the sidewalk behind a new Chrysler just as a shot was fired from the speeding car. The slug went through the window of the Chrysler on the far side and went through the body of the door on the sidewalk side and dropped in the gutter inches from my face. By the time I got to my feet the car was around the corner and gone and I didn't know if it held one person or two, and of course I hadn't had a look at any face at all. Even the car had been little more than a dark blur.

I retrieved the slug that could have ended my days. It was still hot. I wasn't going to be able to tell much from it after it had gone through the heavy door, but my guess was that it had been fired from a .357 magnum. That had been the sound, too.

The blast of a powerful weapon being fired in the cavern formed between two rows of brick buildings in a city street is ear-splitting. You'd think someone would have poked a head out of a window to see what was going on. If anyone peeked, I didn't see them. I had a vision of ten thousand monkeys in their ten thousand tiny cubicles. We've returned to the jungle. Hear no evil, see no evil, speak no evil is the law of the land. But someone was going to notice the bullet holes in the new

Chrysler soon enough. I dusted myself off and walked on. It wouldn't do me any good to get mixed up in a report of gunfire. With my black face they'd make me the guilty party without a second thought. Gotta grab someone.

But who was out to kill me? That was the important question. The gentle fellows from El Honcho? It didn't seem like their way of doing things. I was sure they would enjoy carving pieces off the turkey who'd made fools of them so far, but gunplay was not their usual style.

How about some enemy from the past? I'd made a few, put some pretty mean hombres in the slammer and cost a lot of big-shots important money. But the pro's don't often waste energy on settling old scores. Win a few, lose a few, then move on is more like it with them.

I tried to replay the scene in my head and more and more I had the feeling I'd glimpsed only one person in the car. The Worcester cop? That fit. He was the kind who'd be a loner - a man who hated all black people, who'd been about to relish clobbering a big black man when another jigaboo took the club out of his hands and then nearly castrated him. He'd want to get even. Killing a nigger, in his book, would be more like an act of heroism. He could pin a medal on himself.

He would have had access to the files on the ticket scam. Maybe he had names for a couple of the kids involved. Could he have found out I was working on it? He'd want to nail the two black kids. Suppose he'd been told I was trying to save them. That would make me an obstacle. Additional reason for wanting me out of the way.

Ashad would be off duty now. No way to reach him until tomorrow. Maybe then he'd be able to call Worcester and find out if someone had been assigned to the case and if they had information on the kids we'd identified.

If I assumed that the Worcester cop was working on this I could assume that he'd located me by getting to the big woman in the South End. He must have had Timothy Burgess's name and address. He'd gone there. The 'gross strumpet' had told him where to look for me. He could have seen me going in and out of the taverns on Cambridge Street. If he was watching from a car I wouldn't have been aware of him. A car is good cover in the city, until the quarry wises up. So he'd seen me go into O'Leary's place and he'd waited for me to come out. He was in luck that the short November days ended early so it was dark by the time I emerged.

Then it hit me that if he had the Burgess address he must have some of the others too. I sprinted to the garage where I'd left the rental car and could have been stopped for more than a dozen 'moving violations' before I pulled up in front of Linda's house. Everything was quiet there. I rang. Andy came to the door. He and Jonah and Linda were eating supper downstairs. No one had been there.

I told Andy I wanted to check on Mrs. Reese and would be back in a few minutes.

I went on foot. A dark blue Reliant was parked across the street from her home, two doors down, and I knew it was the one that had gone past when the shot was fired at me.

The door to the house looked wrong. It was closed but it didn't hang the way it should. When I got near I saw that it had been forced. Gently, I eased it open enough so that I could enter. The sound of a voice reached me from somewhere above. It was a steady low drone puctuated by slaps - a heavy hand being laid on the side of an old head.

I went up the stairs three at a time and burst into Leroy's back room before the cop could turn around. He had Mrs. Reese standing against the bureau, leaning back.

"Don't think you 'rahtly' know, do you," he'd been repeating over and over, whacking her with an open hand at the end of each phrase.

He didn't have time to get his hand on his gun. I chopped at the side of his neck with everything I had, paralyzing his right arm. He was turned half way toward me then. I rammed the heel of my left hand up under his chin, lifting him six inches off the floor. He went over backwards and came down smacking the back of his head on the corner of the marble-topped bureau. It stunned him. I took the gun away from him - a .357 mag in a shoulder holdster. He wasn't carrying any other weapon.

Keeping an eye on him, I eased Mrs. Reese into the big arm chair. She was bleeding from the mouth.

"Is anything broken?" I asked her.

She shook her head but couldn't speak. One eye was almost closed.

"Should I get you a doctor?" Again she shook her head. At the same time, I heard someone enter the hallway down stairs.

"Jeeter?" a voice called.

It was Jonah. "Up here." I said.

He appeared in the doorway, a black high-voltage thunder cloud, about to let loose.

The cop was beginning to try to sit up.

Jonah took in the situation at a glance. He went down on one knee in front of Mrs. Reese. "I'm Jonah Johnson," he told her. "Speedy's father. Lemme look inside your mouth."

She opened her mouth. A dental plate had been knocked loose by the cop and it had cut the gums and the cheeks on the inside. As delicately as if he had been lifting a feather off a cushion, Jonah took the false teeth out and placed them on the bureau beside him.

"I'll go for a glass of water and a bowl," he said. "We'll rinse and see if they any damage."

The cop had got into a sitting position, his back against the wall.

"If you get up," I told him, "it will give me great pleasure to knock you down again."

He decided to stay where he was.

Jonah was back in two minutes. He helped Mrs. Reese as she rinsed out her mouth. "Run your tongue around the inside there, Ma'm," he said. "You feel anything wrong?"

"I'll be all right," she said. Without the plate her enunciation was not what it had been.

"I phoned my wife to come over when I was downstairs, Ma'm. I hope it's all right. She'll be here any minute and help you get to bed. See what you need."

Almost as he said it, we heard Linda come in and run up the stairs. She gasped when she saw Mrs. Reese.

"He hit you anyplace but in the face, Ma'm?" Jonah asked.

She shook her head another time. Her mouth must have been hurting badly. There was an ugly swelling over the eye that had closed now.

Jonah picked Mrs. Reese up in his arms the way he might have picked up a piece of Chinese porcelain. There was gentleness in him to equal all the great strength he possessed.

"Where's the bedroom?" he asked.

"Follow me," Linda said, and they went back down the stairs.

I stood over the cop until Jonah returned. I put the heavy pistol on the marble top of the bureau next to the dental plate. The cop was staring at me. His head had cleared. He hadn't spoken.

Jonah came in and stood next to me. "We gonna kill him?" he asked.

"He doesn't deserve such good luck," I said.

"Might take him out to Nut Island and drop him in one of the treatment troughs. He fit in pretty good with all the rest of the shit."

"He'd just get up and walk away and no one would notice."

"Yeah. An' one like him would end up contaminatin' even honest fecal matter."

"What's your name?" I asked the cop.

He spoke for the first time. "None of your fucking business, Nigger."

"Aw he cute, ain't he?" Jonah said. "Lemme kick his teeth down his throat. Awright?"

"Lay one finger on me and you two coons'll spend the rest of your lousy lives in a federal pen."

"Somebody awready lay a finger or two on you, look like. I itchin' to git my turn."

"Give me your wallet," I said. "Either you hand it to me, or I'll take it from you."

He was going to say something more but changed his mind. He pulled his legs under him and reached for a back pocket.

"You move forward one inch," I said, "and you'll be eating all your teeth and two shoes besides. Sit back and hand me the wallet."

"Shucks, Jeeter, you spoil all the fun," Jonah said.

The cop sank back. He held out his wallet and I took it. Inside were about two hundred dollars, credit cards, Social Security card, license and an ID from the Worcester Police Department.

"Ronald P. Morrison," I read. "Patrolman. Born July 9, 1959." There were no photos in the wallet. There was no ring on his left hand.

"He's single," I said.

"He drop outta sight, no one gonna miss him." Jonah was licking his lips.

"Anyone that does notice he's gone will probably be glad about it."

"The whole Worcester PD will be on your black necks in twenty-four hours, if I don't check in."

"Not if you're on sick leave and came to Boston on your own," I said. "I don't think anyone knows you're here except the two of us. And out-of-town, off-duty, out-of-uniform cops who go around shooting holes in new automobiles on Beacon Hill with a .357 cannon don't get much sympathy from local guardians of the peace."

Jonah hadn't heard about any of that before. "You thinkin' we turn him in?" he asked. "Then add breakin' and enterin' in the night time, and assault and battery with grievous injury to an elderly lady?"

"Tempting, isn't it?"

"But still too good for him."

"So what do we do?" I asked.

"Might stuff him down a storm drain at high tide and park a truck on top of it."

Morrison's color was bad, a sallow green, and there was sweat on his forehead. Nobody from Worcester knew he was in Boston.

"What do you know about the kids who pulled off the ticket deal, Ronald?" I asked.

His eyes narrowed as he looked up at me. "Why should I know anything?"

"Because that's one of the reasons for your coming here."

"So?" He thought maybe he had something to bargain with.

"So you got their names, right?"

"That's right. And so did you. You're looking for them too."

"How'd you get their names?"

He knew I wanted something, but he didn't know what. "Off the teletype. Where else?"

"They're all four runaways. What got you started looking at Missing Persons?"

"One of my buddies spotted Timothy Burgess and remembered the bulletin. Then we checked for other kids that had disappeared."

"And you found Leroy Willis and Eric Johnson..."

"And Anthony Morello."

Did he sense that he'd given me a name that I needed?

"They matched descriptions of the four kids at the Centrum."

"And we got positive identification on all four."

"But every one of them got away."

"They had help."

"I know that too," I said. "And the help has some connection with a joint named El Honcho on Tremont Street. Now what do you know about that place?"

"Nothing." But he'd hesitated just an instant before saying it. Time to file it away. He'd never heard of El Honcho before.

Jonah was watching me, listening, wondering what I was up to.

"Let me lean on him a little, Jeeter," he said. "He knows things can help. I'll get them out of him."

I shook my head, picked up the .357, checked the chamber and made sure the safety was on.

"Tell you what I'm going to do, Ronald," I said. "I'm going to let you walk out of here. My only interest in this case is the boys who've taken off. Not to lock them up. To find them and see if they can be brought home and straightened out.

"You have information I don't have. Maybe you can lead me to them. Like it or not, you're going to help me.

"Just so you won't think anything different, I'm going to deliver this weapon, and a report, and the slug you fired at me on Hancock Street, to a prominent lawyer. He will be instructed to turn everything over to the proper authorities if anything happens to any member of Jonah's family, anything at all. Or if you ever even get within sight of Mrs. Reese again. Or if I turn up dead.

"The report will contain signed affidavits relating your invasion of Mrs. Reese's home and your brutal attack on her. There were witnesses to your attack on my life. I've got them." (Might as well make him sweat that even though it wasn't true.) "Your vehicle has been identified. So have you. Now get out of here."

He got to his feet. For a moment he swayed as if he might fall. He was going to have a sore place in his neck for a week. Some of his teeth were loose. And he had a bloody spot on the back of his head where he'd hit the edge of the bureau.

"You going to give me back my papers and money?"

"You gave the money to Mrs. Reese for her visits to a doctor and a dentist tomorrow. Your papers are going to the lawyer who will return them to you if you observe the instructions I've just given you."

"I can't drive without a license."

"So maybe you'll get lucky and be arrested."

Jonah snorted. "And when they book you they can add a charge about 'impersonating a police officer.'" He laughed.

Ronald P. Morrison didn't see the humor of it. He was a young man, but he didn't walk like one anymore. He tripped once on his way down the stairs. We followed him and saw him drive off. Real slow.

24

Linda had put Mrs. Reese to bed and had made her as comfortable as possible. She had two pillows under her head. The bleeding inside her mouth had stopped. She looked little and old and frail but she was tough inside, a lot tougher than the brute who had hurt her.

"You think he comin' back?" Jonah asked.

"Not likely," I said. "But I'll stay here tonight with Mrs. Reese and you two go home and take care of Andy."

"He know where you live?"

"If he did, he wouldn't have tried to bushwhack me on Hancock Street. He would have waited outside my place for a better time."

Linda leaned over and kissed Mrs. Reese on the forehead. "I'll be back first thing in the morning," she said.

"I do thank you. All of you," Mrs. Reese said.

I found a screw driver and a clothespin after they left and whittled some pegs to put in the holes where Morrison had pulled the screws loose while forcing the door. I got it to close more or less securely. Then I phoned Flo and told her where I was.

"Are you all right?" she asked

"Not a scratch on me."

"I wonder how much you're leaving unsaid."

"The only important thing I'm leaving unsaid is...you know..."

"I know. I'm not sure why we both shy away from saying it, though."

"Because the word too easily takes the place of all it can mean."

"Yes. Funny, isn't it." She paused. "We need words to convey meanings, but they tend to become labels on packages whose contents we have forgotten."

She did know. "I'll see you in the morning," I said.

"I'll be waiting for you."

It was a long night. I slept on the couch in the front room where I could hear Mrs. Reese if she needed anything, but I didn't sleep well. I was awake half a dozen times. Once, I heard her get up and go to the bathroom. She moved slowly, not wanting to wake me, not able to get around easily, but I sensed that she didn't want me to come to her aid unless she was helpless. I doubted she ever would be.

I didn't think Morrison would give us much more trouble - not before he was feeling better. He'd probably returned to whatever hotel had given him a room his first night in town. He'd want to soak for an hour in a hot tub and then go to bed. In the morning he'd be aching, but maybe by then he'd be ready to head for El Honcho. I was counting on that.

What would he do for money? Was he wearing a money belt? I should have checked. Without cash he'd have to pack it up and go home. I hoped he'd had some stashed on him somewhere.

25

Toward noon, the next day, I saw him pull up in front of El Honcho in the dark blue Reliant.

I was wearing an ankle-length, torn and stained raincoat and a hat so disreputable old-time Dover Street bums wouldn't have wanted to pick it up. No one was going to recognize me as I stumbled along Tremont panhandling my way toward the nearest tavern.

Morrison got out of his car stiffly. Even bruised and bent, though, there was an arrogance about the way he looked at the area which should have made anyone want to take him down a peg or two.

I slouched onto the steps of a nearby building and pretended to be counting the small change I'd collected to see if I had enough for a bottle. Morrison walked into El Honcho.

I waited. I counted my change three times. Morrison didn't come out.

After more than fifteen minutes I got up and shuffled toward the door of El Honcho, but before I got there a stocky male came out in a hurry and something about him rang a bell for me. 'A man who seemed to have no neck,' Flo had said - the man who had kept one of the kids in Worcester from being caught and beaten. This guy had the look of a former middleweight. He was built like a tree stump. The bridge of his flat nose was at the level of his shoulders, and where there should have been some indication of a neck there was only muscle - right up to his ears.

Something had happened to Morrison. So much the better.

The stocky guy was walking fast in the direction of the Common, looking ahead, then up and down the street, for a cab. There was one parked at the curb where I was standing. I got into the back seat before the driver could tell me to get lost. I took off the hat and the coat and placed them on the seat beside me as the driver watched. I handed him a ten and said, "We're going to follow that character wearing the green sweater. If he gets into a taxi, don't lose him."

The ten disappeared and the meter clicked on. This was a Boston driver who'd been around a long time. He might even know the man we were following. He'd have a make on me too, if I gave him anything to go on.

The man in the green sweater flagged down a cab and five minutes later he got out on Cambridge Street at the bottom of Garden. Without looking at the meter, I gave my driver five more. I'd wrapped the raincoat around the old hat. I jumped out.

My man walked up Garden Street and entered a brick apartment house that had a scuffed red door. Next to me was a building with a vestibule for deliveries and mail. I stepped inside. It was a place to put on the raincoat and hat again and I was able to look through a side light and watch the place across the street. If anyone went in or came out I'd see them. If anyone came through the place where I was standing they were going to ask me to leave.

Nobody came where I was and nothing happened across the street. There was the usual traffic, contests for parking spaces, a matron walking a dog - no pooper scooper. A pair of executive types with phony leather briefcases marched toward the bottom of the Hill, gesticulating, busy looking important.

There had to be a back way out of the building, but I couldn't cover both back and front. If the man I'd followed went out the rear, I'd never catch him. Barging in, however, didn't seem wise.

I waited for over an hour. Maybe the guy lived here. If he did, he might not come out again until tomorrow. But I didn't think he lived here. He had high-tailed it to this building because of Morrison. There was something here he'd come to get - or get out. Was this the place to which the young boys had been coming? I had to know.

Still wearing the raincoat and hat, I crossed the street and put on an act of half-sodden confusion, as if I couldn't remember where I lived. The scuffed red door was locked. No side lights. I pretended to fumble for a key and instead got out a plastic card and easily opened the door.

It led into a dark hallway. One weak bulb burned at the far end. With the street door closed, the building was as still as a morgue.

Over the years I've developed a thief's sense for the presence of another human behind a partition. The street level of this house was empty.

There seemed to be two apartments per floor - so-called efficiencies, no doubt. Playing it safe, I went to the end of the hall and found a stairway to the basement level. If there was a second way out I wanted to know about it. Sure enough, there was a rear door downstairs. It probably led to an alleyway.

There was a basement apartment, too, which utilized all the space not taken by the heating system.

A cheap flush door had a large #1 painted on it and stood ajar. I pushed it open with my elbow. The smell of dirty socks and soiled bedding enveloped me. What had been intended as a sort of livingroom contained four mattresses lying directly on the floor. The adjacent small bedroom had two more mattresses in it. There was no other furniture. No chairs. No tables. A kind of kitchen contained a sink full of garbage, as well as a stove and a refrigerator - open and empty. Next to it was a bathroom. The stink there was enough to turn my gut. I looked anyway.

In the shower was the slumped, fully-clothed body of a kid no more than twelve years old. I touched his cheek. It was as cold as the metal walls of the stall. He'd been dead for six hours at least.

26

"Jeeter, you gotta stop doin' this to me."

Pat Mooney is a detective lieutenant I've known for more than ten years. He's a big rough shrewd Irishman who always wanted to be a dancer. He's still as fast on his feet as anyone I've known.

I'd gone out, located a pay phone and called him to meet me at the building where I found the dead kid. A medical examiner had come with him and a photographer and a technician.

"If I hadn't phoned you, about a week from now someone else would and the job would have been a lot nastier."

I led the way down the rear stairs and showed them how the flush door had been left ajar. Pat went inside the apartment. He followed the same route I had taken and came back out into the basement hall. The photographer and the technician went in and started work. The doctor spent two minutes with the body.

"Looks like cardiac arrest from some sort of overdose," he said. "I'll know for sure after the autopsy." He left. A man doing sprinkler inspections might have shown more emotion. Here was a young person, not much more than a child, senselessly dead. My own insides were churning.

Pat took a deep breath. He wasn't going to comment, but it had hit him hard too.

"Lotta questions need answering," he said. "This is some kind of a crash pad, but the crashers have split. All but one. Whadda you know about it? Whadda you doin' here?"

I told him almost all of it. Maybe I didn't admit doing quite as much damage to the Worcester cop as I had.

"The guy you tailed here, who came out of El Honcho, was maybe the same guy you saw at the Centrum?"

I hadn't told him it was Flo who saw the man. I hadn't mentioned her.

"I think it was the same man," I said, "and I'm wondering if he might be Pedro Rodrigues, now known as Peter Rodgers."

"We can check on that. If he's got as long a sheet as you say he has, we'll have a description of him. Photos too. Incidentally, how come you know so much about him?"

"Sources, Pat. You have to have sources."

"So maybe I don't have to check since you got an inside track already."

"But you will. Rodgers is bad news. Now he's left a dead boy behind him, if the guy I followed is Rodgers. He may have been the cause of the death - directly or indirectly. The same thing could happen to others."

"How do I know he ever had anything to do with this basement? Maybe he's upstairs sleeping in one of the other apartments."

"You'll check that, too, Pat. You'll question everyone in the building to find out everything you can about what went on down here. You'll find out who rented this apartment. I'd like to know if it was Rodgers."

Two cops in uniform came down the stairs. Pat sent one of them to stand at the front door and question anyone who came in. The other was given the job of working his way upstairs, rousting out anyone who was home and getting all possible information on the building, the owner, the real estate agent who handled the place, if one did, and activities in the basement.

Two other men came downstairs, nodded to Pat, and went to carry away the body of the kid in the shower stall. When the technician and the photographer were gone, Pat and I went back into the apartment.

Could Speedy and Leroy have spent a week in a dump like this? They'd lived in homes where they'd had privacy, quiet, care, regular meals. Their homes were clean. This place was an untended stall. The odor of stale bedding and unwashed bodies and urine clung to the walls. What had it been like when there was the animal heat of of six, or more, adolescents in this cramped space?

Candy wrappers and pizza plates, empty soda bottles and milk containers, half-eaten submarine sandwiches and hot dogs were scattered over the floor. Roaches, scavenger armies, retreated and regrouped as we poked through the debris looking for anything that might tell us more about who had been here.

On one of the mattresses, under a still-wet used kleenex, I found two small pills. They were red. The lab man had missed them. Analysis would reveal what drugs they contained, if any.

Over the sink, in magic marker, someone had blocked out the letters IVAR. Both Pat and I stood looking at that for a long time. Was it a name? One of the kids? It sounded sort of Russian. Slavic anyway. Or was it an acronym? Somehow it seemed familiar, but I couldn't think why. It stuck in the back of my mind like a burr on a sweater and I couldn't shake it loose. Sometimes you have to keep from worrying a thought too much. It'll work its way to the surface in time if you leave it alone. I let this one go for the moment.

Pat kicked at a pair of soiled jocky shorts and a baseball rolled out of them. I picked it up gingerly, afraid it might be covered with excrement. It was clean, though, and it was the one Speedy had brought with him from his home - the one that had Wade Boggs' signature on it. I showed that to Pat.

"This belongs to the kid I'm trying to find," I told him. "It was just about the only thing he took with him when he left home. Maybe they cut out of here in such a hurry he didn't have time to look for it in all this clutter. Or maybe something's happened to him. I sure hope nothing has."

But I realized that if he had been in a hole like this for a week something had already happened to him. It didn't need to be fatal. It might even have some beneficial effect. He could have discovered how lucky he'd been before.

Then the other thing clicked into place. I remembered the photos in Speedy's room, the ones over his bureau. Four photos. Four letters in the word IVAR. The left-hand photo had been of Ingrid Bergman - I. The second, a man, an actor from some years ago for the V. Of course! Van Johnson. Then Abbie Hoffman and Richard Burton.

IVAR meant something. It was the kind of thing kids love to put together. I was almost certain it was a club name or a kind of fraternity symbol. We'd find out what it was soon enough.

In the meantime, where had the group gone? I'd been right on top of them and had let them get away. If I'd followed Rodrigues into the building I might have been able to get to Speedy and Leroy. They'd had time to disappear completely now.

The key was El Honcho. I'd have to go there. It wasn't a healthy place for me after what I'd done to the trio in the park. Mooney couldn't go with me. It was Station #4 territory. Not only that. It was definitely a bookie joint and it had the sanction of the station.

Then I remembered Alex Marques. "You need help someday, Senor, you call me."

Alex is as small as I am. Maybe five pounds lighter. Almost as dark- skinned.

He's a pharmacist. Came to Boston ten years ago and set himself up on Washington Street not far from the Dudley Street Station. At first he rented. He worked 'round the clock. Inside of two years he owned the store. But when he started making good money, three bruisers from Southie began hassling him. They wanted a piece of the action and they had a thing about 'Spics.' Alex made the mistake of giving them a few dollars the first time. They were back the next Friday night asking for more and the situation rapidly deteriorated.

I was on a job in the area and met Alex and he told me what was going on. I made a point of being on the corner the next Friday night when the three goons walked into the shop. I followed them in. One of them turned to me.

"Joint's closed for the night," he said.

"The lights are still on," I said.

"Yours'll be goin' out if you don't move it."

He stood between a magazine rack and a wall with shelves holding tooth pastes and shaving creams and all kinds of bathroom products. He was almost as wide as the aisle, had a big gut that was going soft, and muscle-bound arms that were still powerful but would be slow to swing.

His two partners were on each side of Alex waiting for me to leave. One glanced at me, saw how small I was, and turned back to Alex.

"You three are in the wrong part of town," I said. "You can walk out of here quietly and never come back and no one gets hurt."

The lardbelly in front of me snorted. "A dinge and a spickaroo," he said. "Not two hundred pounds between 'em, an' they're gonna hurt someone?" He snorted again. The sound was more like a wet fart, but it came out of his mouth.

I kicked him in the shins. He sagged forward and I put a left into his belly. He whoofed and reached for my arm but he was so slow I had time to pick a spot on the back of his hand to chop down on with my right fist. I heard at least one small bone snap in there. He wouldn't grip anything with that hand again for a while.

He was in close then. I delivered a hard combination deep into his stomach and he doubled over. A single rabbit punch and he was lying on the floor. He didn't even twitch.

The other two were about to rush me. It would have made a mess of the store. Without really hurrying, I took the nine millimeter out of the holdster and pointed it at them.

"Corpses attract cops," I said. "My people don't want them in here and you don't want to be dead. Now you two scoop this bag of shit off the floor and get lost forever. We see any of you in this neighborhood again, they'll find you floating ass-up in the channel."

I stood to one side. They lugged their pal away. They never came back.

So I phoned Alex and told him what I thought we might do. It was going to require a little improvisation, but at least we had a plan and could count on surprise.

About the middle of the afternoon, Alex walked along Tremont and turned into El Honcho. I'd rented a black, older-model Lincoln Continental and was double-parked out front. The string bean with the string tie was not on duty, I was happy to note, and with a chauffeur's cap on, no one had spotted me yet. When Alex entered the shop, I counted a slow ten, left the motor running, and then ambled in after him. As I came through the door he was saying, "Hey, Man, I jus' wanna play a numbah."

They'd sniffed something wrong, thought he could be a plant, perhaps. He wasn't one of theirs and he wasn't a regular even though he fitted in perfectly on looks and accent.

A man stood by the entrance next to me. The one Alex was speaking to was behind a counter. A third man sat on a packing case by a rear door. He was trimming his fingernails with a clipper. Sharp small pieces of horny scale flew into the air at each snick. Some came down in a display case of tired lettuce.

Along the main aisle there was a refrigerated trough with some processed cheese in it, milk cartons, soda. A limited quantity of canned goods rested on shelves. The pretense of being a variety store was adequately maintained. Perishable goods were at a minimum. Fritos and newspapers and chewing gum and cigarettes just about completed the inventory.

"Whatsamatta, Man? You don' trus' me?" Alex asked, raising his voice.

But the guy behind the counter had recognized me by then. He said something staccato, fast, in Spanish, which I didn't catch. I put my elbow into the man beside me, getting him just above the heart. Momentarily he was paralyzed. Alex had taken a dive over the counter and was wrestling with the man there who was trying to get at something strapped or concealed behind the case. I charged the third character who had stood up and was reaching behind him for a blade that was probably in a sheath on the back of his belt. I caught him dead center with my shoulder and we both went through the rear door, shattering it, as a fourth man came up from the back room. He was holding a .38 Police Special in his left hand. I just kept plowing forward, a body for a shield. The fourth guy would have had to shoot his pal to hit me. He hesitated long enough so both of us ran into him. The gun skittered loose and I picked it up.

"Face down," I said. "Arms spread. Legs spread. And don't move."

I backed to the doorway to see how Alex was doing. He was leaning against the wall, a small pistol in his hand. It looked like an Italian piece. The man with whom he'd been wrestling was on his face behind the counter. The one I'd elbowed was seated on the floor breathing with difficulty. Maybe I'd done more damage than intended. You can kill a man with a hard enough blow just above the heart.

Alex made a small circle with index finger and thumb and smiled at me.

I locked the entrance door and turned the cardboard sign around so it said CLOSED instead of OPEN. One at a time, we tied arms and legs of each of the four men and sat them on the floor in the rear room. The one I'd hurt was beginning to breathe normally.

It wasn't going to be very long before someone came to see what had happened. If it was a cop from Station #4, we'd be in trouble.

"All right," I said. "I'll make it short and sweet. Nobody's interested in the numbers racket you've got going here. All I want is one thing. Where do I find Pedro Rodrigues, alias Peter Rodgers?"

The four exchanged looks but no one spoke.

"You can save yourselves a lot of teeth if you give me what I want."

No one even blinked. They were going to be tough and I have never been able to hurt anyone who is defenseless.

Alex reached inside his jacket. He drew out a small flat black case and opened it. Inside was a pair of surgical scissors. There were also two small vials of clear liquid and a hypodermic needle.

He assembled the needle and I saw one of the four men on the floor start to tremble. He was the largest of the group, the one who had carried the .38. Alex had known something I'd forgotten. A lot of very rough macho types have a terror of needles. It's a phobia they can't control. I watched it in Service where some of the most formidable brutes in line for inoculations would keel over like rag dolls before their turn came. We had one of them here.

Alex used the scissors to cut the sleeves of shirts and jackets up to the biceps. Then he loaded the hypodermic.

"Solution to the pro'lem," he said, squirting a few drops of liquid into the air. "Trut' serum."

The guy who was shaking had changed color. His normally dark face had gone gray. His eyes were on the needle and he had started to wet his pants. The stench was going to be overpowering in a couple of minutes.

Alex leaned over him. "You wanna tal my fran where to fin' Pedro?" he asked.

"Don' put no needle in me," the man begged. "I tal you. Pedro gotta place at 68 Myrtle Street on Beacon Hill. Don' put no needle in me. *Por favor.*"

"You theenk he tal the trut'?" Alex asked me.

I waited a moment, watching the guy turn almost green.

"Put it away," I said.

We left the four, tied to each other, in the back room. One of them was not going to remain in good standing. He'd be lucky if he ever found work again in Boston.

They'd get loose before too long, but I had some time.

I drove Alex back to the pharmacy. He kept the small gun. It was a Beretta. Probably no one from El Honcho would find him again. His was a different turf. That's like living in another city, but a weapon is nice to have - just in case.

27

An hour later I was back on the Hill. I couldn't find a place to park. To Hell with it. I left the big wagon where it said Tow Away Zone. Anyone came to tag it, or tow it away, they might think it belonged to a member of the Great and General Court, or to some North End mafioso, which is what I had wanted it to look like. Meter maids, and cops in sidecars, close an eye where the high and mighty pause.

The address was an apartment building of relatively recent vintage, but which apartment was the one that Rodgers rented?

In the foyer were two banks of mailboxes. There was no Rodgers listed and no Rodrigues. There were names like Pakradoonian and Maharaj - no one would pick an alias like that. Periodicals and papers littered the floor. Clearly, many of the occupants of the building were students, judging by the kinds of publications they received. That eliminated several more apartments.

If Pedro lived here - and I was pretty near certain he did - then he had to get a phone bill or an electric bill once in a while. How would he get out of that without a name? "Occupant 3-B", or some such, might do it. But every mail slot had a name on it. Some had two or three. That didn't fit with what I felt was Pedro's type. He'd be a loner in his own place.

One name stuck out for its ordinariness - Roberts. It was for a ground floor rear apartment and Roberts and Rodgers were too much alike to overlook.

There had once been a lock on the inner door to the building that opened by pushing a buzzer in the apartments. It had long since been put out of commission. I walked into the first floor hallway and went to the rear. A radio was playing somewhere upstairs, but apparently many of the occupants of the building were out. I put my ear against the door to Roberts' place and could hear nothing from inside. Instinct told me the apartment was empty. I tried the door. It was locked. The lock had a dead bolt. I wasn't going to be able to get past that.

Stairs led to the cellar. I went down them and found a rear door to the alley and came out between the building and a high brick wall. The ground floor two-over-two windows were just out of reach. I located an empty trash can and stood it upside down under one of the windows. Standing on the can, I would have been able to look through the window into the room, but the shade was down.

There wasn't any screen or storm sash and the only thing keeping the window secure was a simple catch between the upper and lower part.

The high brick wall behind me was partial cover. A looming Ailanthus tree helped. If it hadn't lost its leaves I would have been completely invisible to any and all. But it was November and the tree was bare. I took a chance anyway. No one was leaning out of a window in this weather.

With my pocket knife I was able to whittle away enough of the wood so I could turn the latch.

I pushed up the lower sash and climbed into the apartment. If it was Rodrigues's place, he was going to know that I had been given his address. There was no reason to try to conceal the way I got in. He wasn't going to call the police.

I left the shade down. It was dark inside. All the other shades in the apartment were drawn. This guy had no use for sunlight. Or fresh air. From the ground floor he wouldn't have had much of the former anyway, but a deliberate exclusion of all daylight seems to say something about a person's character. Even if I hadn't already known he was an undesirable type, I would have taken a dim view of him.

I switched on some lights and checked the layout. There was a livingroom, a bedroom, a miniscule kitchen and bath. No one had ever dusted and cleaning had been a rare occurrence. An enormous TV dominated the livingroom. The furnishing were garish, ornate, tasseled - red velvet drapes at the windows, gold flowery patterns on the pillows on the green over-stuffed sofa, paintings in heavy curlicued frames of islands in azure seas. On a table in front of the divan were copies of "Oui" and "Hustler" and "Playboy." In the bedroom, on the wall facing the head of the bed, in living color, was a photo, two-by-three feet in size, that belonged in a class in gynecology. What an interior decorator!

I put a table against the door into the apartment and set a stack of dishes on top of it. If the door were to be opened, there'd be one Hell of a crash to alert me. Then I started taking the place apart.

At the end of an hour and a half I knew there was not one single written record of any kind anywhere in those rooms - no bills, no checking account, no address book, no notes to himself, no phone book, no newspapers. The magazines had been bought at a newsstand. Food came out of a supermarket. This guy was a fanatic about never writing anything down. Or maybe he didn't know how to write.

I was stymied. Short of staking the place out and waiting until he came by - if he ever did - I hadn't gotten any closer to him. There was nothing incriminating on the premises - no weapon, no drugs, not even any cash. I'd counted on finding some sort of lead. I'd come up with nothing.

Would he return for his clothes? Except for a couple of gaudy shirts and one decent dark gray suit, there wasn't much anyone would miss. Still, it's a nuisance having to buy things you've already acquired. Maybe he'd send somebody and not come himself. That figured. He'd be careful. Very careful. I could waste weeks trying to stick with his few belongings.

Perhaps someone in the building would have a line on him. I thought that over. Cop work. Talk with a hundred people. Quiz shop owners in the neighborhood. Mailmen. Meter readers. The owner of the building. The agent.

Nuts!

How about Pat Mooney? By now he would have gone through the building where we found the dead kid. This was a similar shot with a much bigger reason for being thorough. And he had the troops for it. Maybe Mooney had something by now.

I left things as they were, in a mess, and went out through the front door. Not having a key, I couldn't lock it. Anyone would be able to walk in. That had interesting possibilities.

The Lincoln was where I'd left it. No ticket. I should drive around in one of them all the time.

Pat has an office of his own. He didn't keep me waiting.

"Wondered if you'd get back to me," he said, as I walked in.

"I didn't want to harass you."

"You come up with anything?"

I told him I'd paid a visit to El Honcho. Didn't provide any details. Told him it had produced an address. Said I was just coming from there after going through the apartment. It didn't seem necessary to tell him how I'd gained access.

"So you still got nothing."

"I know a good deal more about what kind of man Rodrigues is. He's not going to be easy to nail. He's like a roach in a cellar and will scuttle behind a thousand objects before we corner him. He's a piece of walking slime."

"But you got nothing concrete."

"So I've come to you."

"Yeah. Funny, isn't it. I was about to put out an AP on you."

There was a change in his tone.

"What does that mean?" I asked.

"It means another corpse turned up. You know who?"

"One of the kids?"

He just stared at me. I didn't want to believe it.

"Not one of the kids," he said.

I was able to breathe again, but the way Pat was looking at me, I knew something was wrong. What? Then I had it.

"Tell me who," I said.

"You know, don't you."

"Maybe I've guessed."

"Maybe you didn't need to guess. Maybe you killed him."

"Who, Pat? Who got killed?"

Pat and I have known each other for a long time. An understanding has developed between us. I've helped him as often as he's helped me. He's winked at the way I've done things sometimes, because I've gotten results and because legalities often get in the way of accomplishing what the Law sets out to do. But he hasn't always been happy about my methods.

He would have needed a search warrant to get into the apartment on Myrtle Street, and quite likely he wouldn't have been able to obtain one. Legally, there hadn't been sufficient cause. If he decided to quiz me on it...

"There's this cop comes from Worcester," Pat said. "You told me you stopped him from clubbing your friend Jonah. You didn't say you damned near crippled him for life. I'm told they gave him two months sick leave for what you did to him.

"Other evening we had a report of gunfire on Hancock Street. Witness said a black man almost got it when a dark blue or black Reliant pulled up near him and shot a hole in a parked car. Black man could have been you.

"A dark blue Reliant, registered to a certain Ronald P. Morrison, has turned up on Union Park in the South End.

"Ronald P. Morrison is the name of the Worcester cop. Seems like he might have had reason for wanting you dead. You told me how you caught him beating up on the grandmother of one of the boys you're looking for. You didn't explain how much further damage you did to him when you stopped him that time. Is that when he got a hairline fracture on the back of his skull?

"Then you said you saw him go into El Honcho and you claim you didn't go in but followed the man you think is Rodrigues who led you to the pad where you found the dead kid.

"Now, Old Buddy, Morrison has turned up in a vacant lot on Columbus Avenue. Shot through the heart. A .38 slug lodged against the spinal column."

Pat was still giving me that basilisk stare.

I said, "The gun may have been the one I took away from one of the men at El Honcho a couple of hours ago."

"Got your prints on it then, right?"

I hadn't thought of that.

"Pat," I said, "the gun is in the trunk of the Lincoln Continental I rented. I will gladly turn it over to you so there can be a check on ballistics. And on prints. Alex Marques will confirm what happened and how I got the gun. If it's the gun that shot Morrison and if Morrison was shot yesterday, I couldn't have done it because I didn't have the gun then."

"Lots of ifs in that story. You had pretty good reason for wanting to kill Morrison. He'd already tried to off you. And suppose you killed him with a different weapon, then disposed of the one you say you took away from some guy at El Honcho, and put the murder weapon in the trunk of the Continental?"

"I'm beginning to resent this, Pat," I said. "We've worked together a lot of times over the years. I cut corners every now and then, yes, but I never killed anyone and tried to pin it on somebody else. What's back of this?"

At last he looked away from me. It was as if some bully had been holding my head under water and had suddenly stopped. I was able to appreciate what a guilty party would feel if Pat laid that look on him.

"When I saw the report on a homicide in the South End," he said, "I knew it was the cop you'd told me about. I phoned the captain at Station #4. He put me through to a detective named Bonaparte who's in charge of the case. We exchanged bits and pieces of information. He was not too interested in help. He was most interested in a 'dark-complexioned free lance operator' who'd been 'screwing around' in his territory.

"You're gonna get roasted, Jeeter, by some disagreeable fellows on whose toes you seem to have stomped. I'd like to be certain they can't frame you.

"Just to make matters cosier, the Worcester PD is sending someone to identify the body and to work you over, if there's anything left of you when it's his turn. So don't get huffy with me if I give you a warm up. You're gonna need to be in shape."

His eyes swung back to me. "Some friends are almost more trouble than they're worth," he said.

"Thanks for the 'almost'."

"Yeah. Now lemme get a stenographer and an extra witness and we'll go to the Continental and an officer will remove the gun from the trunk and tag it and we'll hold it until Station #4 brings the slug that killed Morrison here for comparison. If they don't like doin' it my way, they'll have to call in the Attorney General and no way will they avoid blowing their cover on El Honcho."

"Pat, you're a sweetheart."

"Keep your distance."

"Never fear."

I gave him the keys to the car. A stenographer took my statement. An old timer, overdue for retirement, came along and got the gun out of the trunk.

When the others had left, I asked Pat what he'd learned at the building where the kids had been staying.

"Not much," he said. "One tenant had watched some of the kids come and go. They always used the rear door and traveled in pairs, almost always after dark. The two black kids were recent additions. The tenant identified them from photos as Leroy and Speedy. She also identified Timothy Burgess. The others didn't match any pictures we have. And the dead kid remains unknown. According to the autopsy, he suffered from some kind of heart malfunction, a valve with a name I've forgotten, and when he got a little Angel Dust in him, the valve quit and he died. If these kids are foolin' around with that stuff, they may all be dead before long."

"How about who rented the apartment?"

"We located the owner of the building. He had it under management by Minnie Lajoie, an old broad who's been in real estate on the Hill as long as anyone can remember. She said a man rented the place over the phone. He used the name Roberts. She never met him. He paid for three months in advance in cash which an Hispanic-looking man handed her in her office in exchange for the keys. There are almost two full months still paid up."

"Didn't she get an address on Roberts? A phone number? Credit references? Name or names of who would be living in the apartment?"

"I asked her. 'What for?' she said. She said she knew something was fishy the minute he called. She told him if he wanted the apartment to set up a couple of call girls, the operation wouldn't last even one hour and no money would be refunded. He told her he worked in an unofficial capacity with boys from foster homes. Three of them might be sharing the apartment and when he found a permanent home for them, others would take their places. She said she smelled all kinds of rats and thought he'd go somewhere else if she asked for three months in advance. But he didn't. She let him know that if any other tenant in the building was disturbed in any way by whatever went on in the basement, the rental would terminate. He sent the cash to her the next morning. She checked up a couple of times and there were no complaints."

"Do you suppose the kids were being used as courriers?"

"It's possible, but I don't think so."

"Why?"

"Something else has come to light. We been getting a lot of B and E's around the Hill lately. One of my men came to me with a handful of reports. Mostly, small valuable objects have been taken - ivory figurines, jewelry, gold watches. Some worthless stuff has been taken too, and a lot of priceless stuff missed. Amateurs but specialists. And one thing caught my eye."

"What was that?"

"In every case, recently, someone has traced the letters IVAR on a mirror or window, or some other flat surface."

So we had something solid to work with. At last.

Apparently a team of young males was operating in pairs, breaking into apartments and grabbing things they could hide under their shirts or in their pockets. Somebody, almost certainly Rodrigues, was fencing the stuff for them. Perhaps he was providing the addresses to rip off. And maybe he was supplying the boys with drugs in order to keep them dependent upon him.

I tried to understand how a kid like Speedy could get sucked into anything like this. He'd probably never stolen anything when he lived at home. No one in his family would have tolerated any form of dishonesty.

Could that explain it? Was the straight world an enemy in his eyes, a tyrant, an obstacle?

I remembered my own feelings when Jerry and I decided to try stealing back when we were about Speedy's age. It was a way of breaking the rules, an act of defiance, and there was the prospect of having money and a measure of independence as a result. There was one other thing too. While we were doing it, the danger of being caught was a source of excitement. We lived a half hour, or more, of exhilaration, of intensely heightened awareness. It was a high.

"Rodrigues has to find another place for the kids," I said. "Maybe he already has. He will have used the same method he did before."

Pat saw what I was leading up to. "We can't start phoning every real estate office on the Hill asking who's looking to rent a basement pad over the phone. Besides, how do we know he'll stay nearby? He might shift to Brookline, or Cambridge, or the Back Bay, or Winchester, or anywhere."

"That leaves us waiting to spot a series of breaks, somewhere, with small valuables being taken. It could be weeks, even months, before we have something to go on. Meantime, what happens to those youngsters?"

"They could leave their signature again."

"IVAR. That would make it almost too easy."

"Stupid, you mean."

Pat was right. It was plain stupid. Rodrigues must not know they were doing it. If he did, he'd order them to stop. Had the kids become so confident that they thought no one could catch them? Or did one of them want to be caught?

"Can you get a look at reports of all B and E's in the greater Boston area?"

"I can assign someone to it."

"If IVAR shows up again, it could pay off."

Pat nodded. He'd cover it.

28

I turned in the Lincoln and paid the bill. I was about to leave the rental office when three burly Boston cops converged on me. They were in uniform.

The clerk in the office was watching. He looked to be about nineteen. He was wearing a silver Star of David outside his open-necked green shirt.

"Hands against the wall, legs spread," one of the cops ordered.

It would have been suicide to resist. I did as I was told and they frisked me. They took the Walther and my wallet, too.

The cop who held my wallet opened it and checked my ID. Then he said, "You're under arrest. You have the right to remain silent. Anything you say may be used against you."

He hadn't even memorized the reading of my rights.

They put cuffs on me.

"What's the charge?" I asked.

"Murder," he said. "Anything else you'd like to know?"

I turned toward the clerk. "Phone Pat Mooney," I said, and gave him the number to Pat's private line. "Tell him what you've witnessed here."

One of the cops walked up to the clerk. "You ever wanna hold a job for more than five minutes anywhere in the greater Boston area, don't make no call."

The kid had backed up, his eyes flicking from me to the cops and back again.

"Yes, Sir," he said, but I had the feeling he was less intimidated than he seemed.

"Out," the biggest cop ordered, and shoved me through the door.

A cruiser was triple-parked outside, traffic piling up behind it. They pushed me into the back seat and a cop sat on each side of me, meaty haunches mashing me into the smallest space possible. The third officer got into the driver's seat and we took off, sirens screaming and lights flashing.

At Station #4 they threw me into the drunk tank, after confiscating everything I had on me except my clothes, and held me for well over twenty-four hours without booking me. When they got around to it, I was booked as John Doe, D and D. Just an unfortunate mix-up on the part of rookie cops, of course.

What I didn't know was that Pat, thanks to the clerk at the car rental, was already on it. Some heads were due to roll.

That didn't stop anyone from hauling me out of the tank at three-thirty AM. We went straight into a probable cause hearing before a judge who was as good as asleep and so close to senility that he was barely able to follow the directions someone had given him. There were affidavits from Worcester and from persons not present who were alleged to have been attacked and held at gunpoint by me at a place of business known as El Honcho. The papers from Worcester stated that I had viciously beaten Ronald P. Morrison while he was attempting to subdue a rioter.

"Have you anything to say for yourself?" the judge asked. But before I could reply he continued, "I order you held without bail on a charge of first degree murder," and they whisked me off to a cell where I was by myself. At least that was a lot better than being with a half dozen puking drunks. There was no way to communicate with anyone, though. I could only wait. I didn't think it would be long.

The cell was heated and not too dirty. The bunk was hard but they say it's good for the back to lie on a hard surface. I had no trouble sleeping and when I woke up a gaunt angular chap wearing a three-piece suit and carrying a briefcase was stepping into the cell with me.

"Vance Sutcliffe," he said, sticking out a bony hand. "Pat Mooney suggested I find you. Wasn't easy. Some highly irregular measures have been taken in your case. We'll see that a stink rises to noses which will not ignore it. I'm an attorney, as you must have guessed. Let's get the facts in this matter."

He was with me for less than an hour. He seemed to have total recall. His questions were good ones.

When he had what he wanted, he asked me if there was anything I needed. I asked him to phone Linda and tell her what had happened. The same for Flo. He said that had already been taken care of,

"No one is to know my unlisted number," I said, "or the address of my apartment."

"We've been careful not to reveal that information." He'd put a distance between us, now that the questioning was over.

"You've made a few enemies," he said. "Some of them appear to be dangerous. On the other hand, you have some loyal and influential friends. Very few men manage that. I look forward to seeing more of you."

Then he was gone.

I spent three days and three long nights in that cell. Food was brought to me by a cop who could have been deaf and dumb.

The second morning, two men appeared in the corridor. The door between us remained locked. One of the men was an inch shorter than I, but must have weighed nearly two hundred pounds. It wasn't all fat. A lot of it was the kind of padded sinew you could strike with a baseball bat and never crack a bone. Even his bald head seemed to have a layer of muscle under its pink skin. Beady porcine eyes looked out at me through rolling hillocks of flesh.

The second man was in uniform. A cop. But not from Boston. From Worcester.

They didn't say who they were. It was a while before I guessed that the heavy one was the detective named Bonaparte.

"So that's him," the latter said, "a scrawny fucking nigger."

"Let's get the key and find out how tough he is."

"I already tried to get it. He's got protection from higher up."

"Why don't you stand a little closer to the bars," the cop said to me. "You afraid we might mess up some of your kinky hair?"

I was tempted to let him try to grab me. It would have been easy to break his arm.

"He's yellow," the detective said. "A yellow nigger. Probably got his start as a pimp. A big shot becauee he could whip a string of two-dollar whores. That right, Shit-face?"

They were pathetic. Like a couple of school kids trying to provoke me. I crossed my arms, leaned against the wall out of their reach and enjoyed their frustration. They kept it up for ten minutes while I never said a word. Then they went away. I rather hoped the day would come when we'd meet again.

No one else came to see me.

The morning of the fourth day, Sutcliffe came back with a guard. The guard opened the door to my cell and we went out to the desk where I was given all my belongings. Vance drove me back to the IIill.

"We got all charges dropped," he said. "Records of the probable cause hearing were incomplete and obviously falsified. Three persons involved have been transferred. You've still got the same enemies, though, and I'm sure they're no less determined to get you than they were before. Better be careful."

"Thanks," I said. "What do I owe you?"

He was a lawyer and they are a breed apart. There is something fundamentally corrupt about a profession that will put itself on either side of any dispute or crime, provided the fee is right. Did this lawyer sense my reservations?

"Sometimes I need help on a case," he said. "I like to see criminals taken out of circulation. I never defend anyone I believe is guilty."

He had read my mind.

"I'd like to be able to call on you, if you'd permit me."

It could have been just a smooth line, but I didn't think so.

"Any time," I said, and gave him my hand.

29

Flo came out of the back room as I opened the front door to the apartment. She was wearing an old full-length checkered house coat. Her hair was tied up the way she did it when she took a shower. It gave her wide face a far-eastern look.

We stepped toward each other and met at the center of the livingroom. She was as fragrant and lovely as lilacs, and the jailhouse smell on me made me shy. She put her arms around my waist in spite of it. I felt like some old derelict with my four-day beard, unwashed, unkempt.

She took a deep breath and let it out slowly. I felt her body relax and go soft and yielding.

"I can accept it," she said. "I can work when you're away and not squander energies in futile worrying. But the relief when you reappear is like a dam bursting. Thank heaven, you're back."

Gently, I pushed her away from me. Her eyes were full of tears. "Let me shower and shave," I said. "I'm not fit to be near as I am."

I went into the bathroom and stripped and spent half an hour lathering and rinsing, shampooing, getting the last of the stench of vomit and cigarette smoke and disinfectant and sweat out of and off me. I shaved the coarse stubble from my face and rinsed again and brushed my teeth at last and began to feel whole once more. And human. The caged animal part that even a few hours in jail bring out receded, but I knew I would never be able to erase the mark it had left on me.

Flo stood waiting for me beside the bed. I undid the belt on the house coat and she turned away as I lifted it from her shoulders and dropped it on a chair. She had nothing else on.

It was full daylight. Sunlight fell through the window on her back. I let my hands move on her lightly, following the shifting mounds and hollows that made her body such a thing of wonder. Shivers of pleasure ran on her where my fingers touched.

Slowly, she turned to face me, her belly brushing and lifting me before pressing against me. We held each other, the need to reject isolation as great as the need to answer desire.

I've been too much alone in my forty-one years, have raised barriers to feeling. My defenses down, unprotected from emotion, I found myself alive in a way I hadn't known before, awareness doubled, everything Flo felt as keen and essential as everything impinging on me.

One aspect of love, after all, is sensing what another feels and responding to it. Was a difference in color an added reason for not taking for granted what should each time be new? Did that account for the fact that our love-making often proceeded slowly, almost cautiously? Flo paused sometimes and looked at my blackness and put her palm on me as if testing, the way one might reach for an unfamiliar fabric to feel the texture of it, some special smoothness or softness or durability. We were discoverers, both of us, as all new lovers are, but there was an extra dimension to our explorations.

Not until late in the afternoon did we start talking. She wanted to know everything that had happened to me. In telling her, I came to see more clearly what was important and what was of little significance. I could forget those two clowns who had taunted me when I was behind bars. They'd trip themselves up without my help sooner or later. But Speedy and Leroy were in danger and somehow I had to get to them without losing more time.

"You mentioned something the cop from Worcester told you - the one that's dead. He gave you another name."

"Anthony Morello. Sure. He must have been one of the four at the Centrum."

"And you haven't tried to find out anything about him."

It was true. If he was one of the kids who'd been involved in the ticket caper he would have known Speedy for a while. At least that seemed likely.

I got on the phone and luckily Ashad was still at his desk.

"Morello?" he repeated. "That one just came in a couple of days ago. But today someone called in and said he was back home."

"Do you have an address?"

It was on Joy Street. Only a few blocks away.

By the time I got dressed and had something to eat it was after five and dark out.

"Be careful," Flo said. "I'll be waiting."

I kissed her. "Keep the door locked," I said. "I don't want anything to happen to you."

The address on Joy Street was near the bottom of the hill, almost across from the old police station. Apartment number three had the name Morello on it. I leaned on the buzzer. There was no answer. I pressed it again and kept pressing until at last someone came into the hallway and looked through the glass door at me. He was fiftyish, stocky, almost bald. He had a wide jaw full of even strong teeth. He breathed heavily through a partly opened mouth.

"Who you want?" he asked.

"I'm looking for Anthony Morello," I said. We had to raise out voices a little, but not too much.

"He ain't here."

"Does he live here?"

"Who wants to know?"

"I'm a friend of Speedy Johnson."

"Of who?"

"Speedy Johnson," I said, speaking more loudly.

There must have been some sound behind him. He turned and said, "Get back inside."

But a face came out of the darkness at the rear of the hall and a skinny kid was there staring at me.

The older man said, "What's your name?"

"Jeeter," I said.

The kid came up beside the man. "It's all right," he said. "Let him in."

They opened the door. I followed the kid as he led the way into the apartment. The heavy-set man was close behind me.

We walked through an untidy livingroom into a kitchen with a formica table and four wooden chairs around it. The sink was full of dirty dishes. A pot full of some kind of tomato sauce was bubbling on the gas range and a skillet next to it had sausages sputtering in it.

The man turned the gas way down under each and said to sit down at the table. The kid and I sat down, but the man stood behind me and a little to one side.

"You're Anthony Morello?" I asked.

The kid nodded.

"And you know Speedy?"

"Yes."

"Was Leroy Willis with you, too?"

"Just hold on a minute," the man said. "I ain't too sure who you are yet."

"It's all right, Unc. Speedy told me about Jeeter. Jeeter and Speedy's old lady were close once."

"He's some kinda fuzz."

"He's a PI."

"So he's trouble."

"Unc, Speedy and Leroy are friends of mine. They're gonna get hurt. Maybe Jeeter can help."

"What about me? You don't give a damn I been takin' care of you all these years."

"Maybe you'd taken better care I wouldn't have got mixed up in all this."

"Why you little punk, I'll show you..."

The man took a step toward the kid and raised his hand. I grabbed his arm and twisted. "Wait," I said. The man tried to throw a left at me so I turned his arm over and he screamed. He was slow and flabby and old. It was no contest. "Now you sit down," I said, and I dropped him into a chair.

I sat down again. The kid had backed up, overturning his chair. He righted it and sat, leaning against the wall, well out of reach of his uncle. The uncle was massaging his shoulder, murder in his eyes as he looked at me.

"Mr. Morello." I said, "I'm not interested in any activity of yours, unless it affects the boys I'm looking for. Now you just keep quiet unless I ask you something."

I turned to the kid. "Tony," I said, "I want to know everything you can tell me, starting with how you first met Speedy and Leroy. When was it and where?"

He was only a youngster, maybe even a year younger than the other two. His skin was bad. It had that off-yellow tint of the person who has almost never been out in the sun and it didn't look as if he had ever eaten the right kind of food. But if I'd understood, it had been his uncle who had raised him. Probably he was a man with no education or trade. Maybe he'd done his best with what he'd had. Was the kid an orphan? Perhaps the uncle had loved him once.

"Speedy and Leroy got bused to the same school with me this year."

Tony's voice hadn't changed yet, he was that young, or that immature. It was soft and high, with something musical in it.

"We made friends from the first day. I'd never known, you know, any black people before, but both of them were real nice to me. When we found out we all liked the game of Dungeons and Dragons, that did it. We hung out together all the time. Another guy, Burgess, was with us and he knew a old wino named O'Leary, lives in a cellar on Hancock Street. We used to play the game there. O'Leary's a faggot. He tried to get close to me an' I told him to forget it. He said that was all right. He's kind of a sad old guy. I think him and Burgess make out. In fact I know they do. So what? Burgess isn't very smart. He has hardly any friends. If him and O'Leary like each other, what's so wrong?"

Morello clenched his fists. "I ever get my hands on him, I'll break his neck."

"Then they'll lock *you* up," Tony said.

"So there were four of you," I said. "How did you get into this other thing?"

"Well..." he looked his uncle in the eye..."Unc runs numbers and often he asks me to help out. I carry slips for him sometimes."

Morello started to get to his feet. I put a hand on his arm.. "Mr. Morello," I said, "I've already told you. I don't care about this part of it. No one is going to hear about what you do from me. You could be the biggest numbers man in town. That doesn't interest me. Now take it easy."

He calmed down, but he wasn't happy.

"So I was going to this joint called El Honcho. It's down on Tremont in..."

"I know where it is, Tony."

"Yeah. Well...a guy in there started gettin' palsy with me. I figured him for another one like O'Leary, but that wasn't his thing. He gave me a line about how a clever kid like me should be making real money. I strung him along and found out he had a set-up where several guys had an apartment he rented for them and they really lived it up in return for stealing small things from empty pads. It was like being in a sorta club, but you had to pull off one theft on your own as a kind of initiation.

"I told him I had three friends I'd talk to about it. He wasn't pushy. Just said he had a place empty where we could live our own lives. We'd have money. Anything we wanted. He knew how to make it sound pretty good.

"When I told the others, Burgess couldn't wait. Leroy and Speedy weren't too sure. I explained that it meant we'd have a place of our own and we could quit school. That was one thing we all agreed on - school was a drag - and when I mentioned that we had to steal something on our own in order to get into the club, everybody started thinking what it could be without considering if it was right or wrong. That was funny, wasn't it? I did it too.

"It was Speedy who had the best idea. I think he's a genius. Honest. He was learning graphics and..."

"He printed some phony tickets."

"You know about that?"

"I found out. Was it just you and Speedy and Leroy and Burgess who went to Worcester?"

"Yeah. And we made out, too."

"People got hurt."

"It was wild, Man. But you're right. And Speedy's folks saw him. You must have been with them."

"I was. Was Rodrigues with you?"

"You mean Roberts. His name is Roberts. Yeah. He drove."

"Roberts is one of the aliases he uses. His name used to be Pedro Rodrigues and he has a mile-long criminal record under that name. Then he changed it legally to Peter Rodgers. Now he's calling himself Roberts. There may be other names he uses too. So he set you up in an apartment on Hancock Street. Is that right?"

"Right. And we had a party to celebrate the deal we'd pulled off in Worcester. He said we had to keep it quiet. He brought us a little Sony radio and a huge chocolate cake and a gallon of ice cream. There was milk, too, and he put something in the milk that got us all high. We didn't know he was going to do that. At least I didn't.

"There were two other kids there and they knew what was going on."

"Who were they?"

"One we knew only as Chris. He was the one that..."

"He was the one that died, wasn't he?"

"Yeah. I think he was already hooked on something. He was moody. He'd just lay on his pad all day long except when he had a snort of something. I think it was coke. Then he'd be cool for a while and smile and make a joke sometimes."

"Who was the other kid?"

"We called him Hammerhead. He had, well, I might as well say it. His pecker had a big knob on the end of it so we teased him about it. He'd get real embarrassed, but every time he'd take a leak we'd ask to see the hammerhead."

"Did he have any other name?"

"I think his name was Benny Cornman."

"What happened to the money you cleared on the tickets?"

"Roberts - or whatever his name is - let each of us keep a hundred bucks and he took the rest and said he'd put it in a trust fund for us. He was real pleased with the way we'd worked that one. Chris and Hammerhead didn't get anything out of it except the party, 'cause they weren't in on it."

"You didn't know you were going to be in an apartment with several others, did you?"

"No. We didn't like it either. And the place was nothing like what we'd expected. It was real crummy. I guess the other kids were there to show us the ropes, though, 'cause the very next night after the party, we started going out. Roberts told us where to go and what to look for and never to take anything we couldn't fit in a pocket or under a jacket. Usually, the next day, one of us would drop off the stuff at El Honcho, or at another place on East Brookline Street."

"So what Roberts has is a team of juvenile thieves working for him. He must have some way of spotting places whose occupants are away and where there are things of value. How did you get in?"

"Usually we went up a rear fire escape and pried open a window. Or taped the glass and broke it to reach the catch. Hammerhead's an expert."

"What about the letters IVAR? What do they mean?"

He smiled. "That stands for the Invisible Army. We all wore dark clothes and worked at night. It was fun, in a way. And exciting."

"And pretty soon everyone becomes drug-dependent if Roberts plays his cards right."

"Yeah. Speedy saw that right away. He said we should cut out after the second night."

"Why didn't you?"

"I don't know. Maybe it was because it would have been like admitting we were wrong, that we should have stayed to home and never left."

"But you got out anyway."

"It was the thing with Chris. Roberts left him some stuff he called Crystal. He goes, 'See, it's even got your name. It must be for you, Chris.'

"So Chris tried some the next day and it didn't seem to do anything for him at first. He just got quiet. We'd ask him what it was like and he wouldn't answer. He didn't seem to hear us. Then later, he backed up against the wall and held his hands in front of him as if he was trying to stop something from coming at him. His eyes began looking at each of us like we was some kinda monsters. He was scared. Really scared. He was seein' something that wasn't there and was fighting it off, kicking his feet and pushing with his hands and saying, 'No, no, no.' When we tried to hold him and tell him it was all right, he screamed. He was crying and shaking. Then he went all rigid and quit breathing and his face turned sorta blue-purple and in just a couple of minutes he was dead."

Morello got up slowly and filled a glass with water at the sink and drank it. "Anyone else?" he asked

Tony shook his head.

"No thanks," I said. "Then what did you do, Tony?"

"We didn't know what to do. We were all scared by then. Hammerhead said when Roberts came by he'd know what to do. Burgess said we should wait till nighttime and carry Chris out in the alley and leave him there. I said I was getting the Hell out. We were all still arguing when Roberts came in.

"Roberts told us we had to move, pick up our stuff and get out fast. That was before he saw Chris. When he saw him, he said something in Spanish. Then he took Chris under the armpits and hauled him into the shower stall and pulled the curtain on him. After that, he didn't give anyone time to do anything but run. He gave us an address on Shawmut Avenue and said he'd meet us there. He sent us out the back way, like always. I was with Speedy. Leroy was with Burgess. Hammerhead was by himself. Roberts had taught us to travel in pairs or alone. I told Speedy I was through. He said he was, too, and to Hell with Shawmut Avenue, but he was going back for his baseball. I told him he was nuts, but he went anyway and that's the last I saw of him. I haven't seen any of the others since then either."

"You came back here and have been staying here?"

"Yeah."

"And Roberts hasn't tried to come here?"

"No."

"The police have an order out to pick him up and they're going to be questioning you about him sooner or later. Roberts might want to keep you from talking."

"I know."

"Nobody gets in here without I let 'em in.", Morello said.

"You can't stay here all the time, though. Anyway, you work for Roberts."

"Not no more I don't."

"What do you plan to do?"

"That's my business."

He was a stubborn ignorant man, but he was probably right to keep his plans to himself. Maybe he and Tony could move to Chelsea or East Boston and keep running numbers there, or someplace where he had relatives or connections. Roberts wouldn't have time to go looking for them. He was going to be on the run himself - until he got caught.

But what had happened to Speedy? And Leroy? I had the address on Shawmut Avenue. There could be a lead there. But if Speedy had decided to get out, why hadn't he shown up at his home? I had a feeling he was in more trouble than ever.

31

The house on Shawmut Avenue was a brick building sitting directly on the sidewalk. There were no bells at the front door. No names. No glass so you could look into the hallway - or so anyone inside could look out. I knocked politely once and when there was no reply I knocked again with a certain amount of vigor. Nothing stirred within the building. I stepped into the street and looked up at the windows as quickly as possible. On the third floor, curtains moved. Someone had seen me. I went back to the door and gave it a pounding. No one was going to open it.

Farther down the street was a vacant lot. I walked through it and found my way to the back of the house whose address I had. A scruffy brown dog was worrying a garbage bag near the rear door. The door was unlocked so I went inside. Trash cans lined the hallway. Several were overflowing with rubbish and two rats sat atop one of them impertinently eyeing me. They didn't even jump down when I walked past them.

A door stood open to my left. I looked in. It was another crash pad like the one on Hancock Street - mattresses on the floor, a litter of soda cans, cigarette butts, candy wrappers, magazines. But the occupants were gone. The bathroom was empty. There wasn't any shower stall. No refrigerator or stove. If any of the kids I knew about had been here, they were gone now.

I had my gun in my right hand as I went up the stairs. The halls were unlighted and foul-smelling. On each landing I paused and listened. There was no one living on the two first floors. On the third, in front, I could tell that someone was there. Even if the curtain hadn't moved a few minutes earlier, I would have sensed it.

I stood to one side and knocked once, sharply. There was no response.

"Open up," I said, "or I'll break down the door."

Silence.

"I'm armed," I said. "I'll come in firing if you don't open the door."

A chair scraped and shuffling footsteps approached.

"I open the door now," a woman's voice said. "You don' shoot, please."

I stood back as two bolts were withdrawn and the door swung open. An old woman stood there, stooped, very dark-skinned, short and heavy. Her eyes were on my gun but her face was impassive. Looking past her, I could see that the room was empty except for some decrepit furniture.

"Let's go inside," I said.

She turned and went ahead of me. The room we entered had a chair by the window, a four-poster bed with one of the posters missing, a prie-dieu with a plaster Jesus on it painted blue and gold. On the wall hung a Sacred Heart.

There was a three-by-four kitchen to my left. Empty. Off it was a toilet. Everything was clean. No one was concealed here. I went back to the apartment door and closed it. The old lady had returned to her chair by the window and was watching me.

"I'm sorry to disturb you," I said.

"Tha's all right. You can put away the gun. I don' make no trouble."

Her voice was low and rasping, but it was calm. She was one who had always waited, served, accepted, faith her only bulwark against cruelty and injustice. I'd known others like her among the Puerto Rican women in this part of town. They were the slaves of their men - fathers, husbands or sons, it made little difference.

I put the gun in the holdster and leaned against the bed.

"Some boys stayed in the basement for a while," I said. "Will you tell me about them?"

"Differen' boys stay in the basemen' differen' times."

"Who were the ones most recently?"

"One is black. They call him Leroy. Two are white. I theenk Benny an' Teem."

That would be Benny Cornman and Timothy Burgess.

"How long did they stay?"

"They come in the night. I fix them some soup. Before morning they are gone."

"Did anyone come to see them?"

"I wouldn' know."

Was she holding back?

"What is your name, Senora?"

She looked at me and didn't reply.

"Are you the mother of Pedro Rodrigues?" I asked.

She ducked her head and said something in Spanish. It could have been, "May God forgive me."

"Pedro came here, didn't he?"

She nodded. "He come here. He is very angry. He curse me. He curse his own mother." She raised her eyes to the Sacred Heart on the wall - a gaudy gory replica of that bloody organ. "He ac' like I the cause of all his troubles. For the gift of life to him am I to be cursed? Did I make him what he is?"

"He came here and he took the three boys away with him?"

"Two he send away. The black one he take with him."

"Did he have a car?"

"Yes. Very old car."

"Do you know what model? What make?"

"I don' know cars. This one though have a torn roof. You know? Top you can roll back."

"A convertible."

"Tha's it. And on one side is a torn - a tear. Mus' be cold inside. An' wet."

Why was she telling me all this? Did she want him to be caught?

"Do you think that Pedro will come back here?"

"He don' come back now. He use me. Make me feed many boys. Some no good at all. Now there is trouble for him. He forget me now."

"Did the black boy, Leroy, go with him willingly?"

"They talk about someone. Some fran."

"Speedy?"

"Yes. That the one."

"So Leroy got in the convertible with Pedro and they drove away?"

"Tha's right."

"Where would they have gone?"

"I theenk Rutlan'."

"Rutland Vermont?"

"I don' know Vermon'. Rutlan' Street, I theenk."

Did this guy have another apartment on Rutland Street? Or could it be Rutland Square? He should have been in real estate.

"Senora Rodrigues," I said. "If Pedro doesn't return, will someone take care of you?"

"I don' know wat will 'appen to me."

"May I send someone to you to help you out?"

She stared at me.

"Has Pedro always given you enough money to take care of yourself?"

"Sometimes."

"Have you any money now?"

"Wy you wan' to know?"

Did she think I intended taking it away from her? What a life she must have led.

"I want to be sure you'll be all right until someone can come here to give you a hand."

"I am all right."

"I'll see that someone comes soon."

I turned to go. She said, "Please." I turned back. She was looking deep into my eyes. "You will not shoot my son, I pray."

"I'll do everything I can to avoid that," I said.

"I thank you," she said, and she made the sign of the cross.

I left the apartment. I hoped that when someone came to help her she would open the door.

$\mathcal{I}$t was a little after eight PM. In a corner store I found a pay phone and called Flo to tell her where I was, but before I could say anything, she said Linda had been trying to reach me. "They're holding Speedy for ranson," she said. "Call Linda right away so she can give you details." And she hung up.

Linda must have been standing with one hand on the phone. The first ring had barely begun when she answered. Her voice was high, ready to break.

"Linda," I said. "You had a demand for ransom. Tell me about it."

She took a deep breath that caught with a sob before she began speaking.

"Oh Jeeter. Someone has Speedy. A man called. He said, 'We got your boy. You wanna see him again, get fifty thousan' dollars. I call you back.' What are we going to do?"

"Have you notified the police?"

"No."

"I'll do it. I know who to call. When did the man phone you?"

"But he told me not to call the police or he'd kill Speedy."

"Linda, Speedy's chances are better if we get everyone we can working on this."

"He's probably been killed already." Her voice had gone up another three notes.

"That's not so," I told her. "Kidnappers may kill after they get the money they demand, but if they don't have some kind of proof the victim is alive they risk losing their chance to get the cash. How long ago did you get the call?"

"It was around noon today."

"Did the man say how long you had to raise the money?"

"No."

"Was the voice Spanish-sounding?"

"I think so. It had a high sort of sing-song way. But it was cold. Unfeeling."

"It wasn't a tape, was it?"

"Oh no. He answered when I asked where Speedy was."

"What was his answer?"

"He said, 'Jus' get the money. Then I tell you.'"

"Was there anything else about the phone call? Could you hear any sounds in the background?"

"I don't remember anything. I don't think so."

"So he'll be calling back. I'll see a tap gets put on your phone. You'll have company soon. We'll get federal help on this. Is Jonah there?"

"He's at the bank."

"Can he raise fifty thousand?"

"He thinks he can."

"Look, Linda. We need time. Is Jonah asking for a loan on your home?"

"Yes."

"The bank isn't going to give him cash without a mortgage."

"Jonah's boss says he'll sign for him."

"Let's not give out that information. When you get the next phone call, you, or Jonah, should say there has to be a title search and the mortgage has to be recorded at the Registry before the bank will turn over the money. This could all be done in one day, if anyone ever really wanted to do it that quickly, but usually bankers and lawyers take much longer in order to make it seem as if their exorbitant fees are justified. Try to get three days. Settle for less if you have to. Do you understand?"

"But the longer we wait, the greater the chance that Speedy will be hurt or killed."

"Not unless it's dragged out a lot longer. I think I know the street where Speedy is being held. With some time, and the kind of help I can get now that this is a federal offense, we should be able to reach Speedy before anything happens to him. Our best shot is before the money changes hands. Believe me."

My next call was to Pat Mooney. He promised that technicians would be at the Johnson house within twenty minutes to tap the phone there and record all incoming calls. The FBI would be on the case within hours.

I didn't tell Pat where I was headed because I didn't want Rodrigues to see a lot of plain clothes cops in the neighborhood - if he was holding Speedy on Rutland Street. It was well after dark now and I could pass unnoticed. I knew that part of the South End as well as anyone else alive.

It took me less than half an hour to locate the convertible with the rip in the rag top. It was parked on Tremont in front of a high building that was taken over by a militant group in the 60's. Unless Rodrigues had other vehicles, he was nearby.

Rutland Street, between Tremont and Shawmut Avenue, is mostly residential now. There's a large neighborhood building there with what was once a beautiful courtyard and garden, and there is still one vacant lot where a hideous In-fill building once stood like a blasted bunker. It never was occupied and has since been razed. But most of the houses are now privately owned. Many have been tastefully remodeled.

I shuffled along the street looking as aimless and harmless as possible, checking each facade for signs of lights and occupancy. I could eliminate most of the houses without any hesitation. Young couples with children lived in some. I saw business types and executives entering and leaving others. In rooms where the shades or drapes weren't drawn and lights were on, I saw interiors which had been re-habed in ways that precluded the presence of a Rodrigues.

Going through the alleyways behind each side of the street, I was able to exclude many more dwellings from the list of places where someone like Rodrigues could be holding a fourteen-year-old black kid prisoner.

By ten o'clock I was pretty sure the only likely house was one that backed up on the alley between Rutland and West Concord Street. It was in serious disrepair. A dim light was on in the front hallway. Nobody had gone in or out while I was watching.

I went around to the alleyway. A dog, behind a chain-link fence, growled at me on the corner, but he'd seen me three times already and was getting used to me. The rear of the suspect building was full of junk and filth and weeds. An alley light, three houses away, threw elongated brush shadows against the back door. I tried the door but it felt as if it had been nailed shut. A window at hip height was less of a problem. I pulled down on the upper sash and slowly the catch bent up and over and came out of the lower section. Years of rain water running down the rear facing of the building had rotted the wood. I pushed the upper sash back into position and lifted the lower half of the window and stepped inside.

Street sounds became only a whisper, once I was indoors and the window was down again. The building was as cold as a tomb. And as silent.

I had a pencil light with me. It was enough to keep me from stumbling over the few pieces of furniture I saw.

One room at a time I went through the house. Closets, stairwells, landings - I looked everywhere. Nothing in the basement. Nothing at street level.

The place had been a rooming house for many years, it seemed. Maybe someone had bought it recently and was waiting for financing before remodeling. Did Rodrigues work with someone who had a real estate office? If I was right, and this was another house to which he had access, he had to have a connection with a broker, or someone of the sort. On the Hill there was Minnie Lajoie, but she certainly wasn't in cahoots with him. A management firm? He, or someone he knew, could be caretaker.

On the second floor I stopped abruptly. I heard something. A muffled voice and a thump. It came from overhead. Someone was upstairs. I had my gun out as I crept up the next flight to the third floor. A hall bathroom was between a big front room and two rear rooms. Its door was closed. The noise came from in there. It could be a trap but I didn't think so. What I was hearing was too much like the sounds a person makes when gagged. Cautiously, I opened the door and directed the thin sliver of light around the interior of the bathroom.

In the tub, on a narrow mattress, bound and gagged, was a black kid. It wasn't Speedy.

I shut the door so nothing would show outside and flipped the light switch. Both of us blinked. The kid in the tub was Leroy. He was not in good shape. I untied the gag and undid the plastic-coated phone wire that bound his wrists and ankles. He stunk. He'd wet his pants and it had almost dried. He'd been there a long time. He tried to speak but his mouth and throat were so dry he only croaked. I started water running in the sink as he got to his feet. There was no glass available.

"Make a cup of your hands and drink some water," I said.

Before he did that he pulled up the cover on the toilet, unzipped his pants and urinated. After that he got some water into his mouth and drank. He was stiff and sore and so cold his deep black color had turned a dusty gray. I'd seen an overcoat in a closet on the first floor.

"Stay here a minute," I told him. I turned off the light and went to get the overcoat. He was jogging in place when I got back upstairs. He put on the overcoat and began to feel a little warmer.

"Are you Jeeter?" he asked.

I nodded.

"Have you found Speedy?"

"I thought I was going to find him here. Do you know where he is?"

"Roberts told me he was in this house, but when we got here he tied me up and left me. I don't know where Speedy is."

"Do you think Roberts is coming back here?"

"I did for a while. You wouldn't think he'd just leave me here to die. But I was beginning to believe he might. I don't know."

If Roberts did come back I really wanted to be the one to greet him. But suppose he never did? I needed help.

"Let's get out of here," I said.

Leroy was only too happy to do that.

We went out the same way I'd come in. Then we walked through the alleyway and around to Rutland Street.

"Did Roberts bring you in through the front door?" I asked.

Leroy said he had.

I didn't want to ask it of him, but I didn't want to take any chances either. We were diagonally across from the house and away from the street light.

"Look, Leroy," I said. "I've got to phone to get someone to cover this place in case Roberts reappears. I'm going to leave you here in the shadow just to watch the entrance until I get back. I won't be more than ten minutes. Can you do that for me?"

He looked at me. "You know my name?"

"I know a lot about you, Leroy, and I'm going to get you and Speedy out of this mess, but we've got to nail Roberts too. His real name, incidentally, is Rodrigues."

He was beginning to shake all over. He needed something to eat and a hot bath. "Just don't be too long," he said. "Please."

I shuffled off to the corner and found a pay phone. For a split second I didn't recognize the gruff tense voice that answered.

"Jonah, this is Jeeter. Is Pat Mooney there?"

"Jeetcr! Have you found Speedy?"

"I've got Leroy and I think Speedy is nearby. Let me talk with Pat, if he's there."

Pat got on the phone. "Where are you?" he asked.

"I'm on Tremont Street in the South End, near the corner of Rutland. I need two men, Pat. They should have radios with them and they should be good men who know how to become part of the background. Inconspicuous. I need them to watch two places where Rodrigues may show up. I don't want to spook this guy. You might arrange to have a car standing by on the corner of Mass Ave in case we spot him. And send the two men in a car with a driver so he can pick up Leroy and take him home. He needs a steaming hot bath and soup and food. Desperately. I'll meet the car by the Methodist church on the corner of West Concord Street. Okay?"

"You've got it."

"Any word yet?"

"Nothing. But we're ready."

"Is someone with Mrs. Reese?"

"Two of the best."

"Tell her to start filling a tub for Leroy."

"Gotcha."

I walked back to where I could signal to Leroy. He joined me and we went to the corner of West Concord Street by the church. We had only just arrived there when a dark Chevvy pulled up. Two men got out.

"You Jeeter?" one of them asked.

I told him I was.

"Parsons," he said. "And this is Stillwater. FBI."

"Good," I said. We didn't shake hands. I put Leroy in the front seat of the car. The driver sniffed and was about to say something.

"Take this kid home to Mrs. Reese," I said. "He was bound and gagged for twenty-four hours in a bathtub in an unheated house. Treat him as if he were your own."

Leroy looked at me before I slammed the door. He was shivering so he could hardly open his mouth. "Thank you," he said.

"I want to talk with you when this is all over," I told him. "Don't take off again."

"Don't worry," he said. He tried to smile.

I showed Parsons where Rodrigues's car was parked and he found a place on the other side of the street from which to watch it.

Stillwater came with me and we headed for the alleyway behind the house where I'd found Leroy. "You think

Rodrigues is in the neighborhood?" he asked.

"His car is here and his mother said this is an area where I should look for him."

"What's this about his mother?"

"I found her on Shawmut Avenue. He used her to feed some of the boys he kept on his string, from time to time."

"Suppose Rodrigues has killed the Johnson boy and isn't anywhere near here?"

"We still have to watch these two places in case he is here, or decides to pick up his car, or comes back for Leroy."

"Why not cordon off the area and do a house-to-house?"

"No good."

"Why?"

This prick was beginning to bug me. "Because if he's here, we'd alert him and he'd be holding Speedy hostage before we could get close. Or he'd kill Speedy and slip through your lines. Or maybe he or Speedy or both aren't here at all and the word would be sent to him we were after him with an army and he'd leave the state. He's got to show himself soon. He's got to set up a way of getting the money. He'll have to make a phone call. Maybe two calls. As long as we keep quiet and watch enough places we'll spot him."

We'd reached the rear of the house. "Now, if it's not too much trouble," I said, "I'd like you to take up a post inside this house and if Rodrigues shows up you can be a hero."

I put him through the basement window and rather hoped he'd freeze his ass off and never see anyone.

By seven the next morning, though, I was the one with the frozen butt. Maybe I wasn't the only one. I'd prowled the neighborhood hour after hour. Nothing. No sign of Rodrigues. Nothing to indicate that Speedy was around anywhere. If he was tied up and stashed in a tub somewhere without food or water or heat, his life could be endangered by now.

Two men came to relieve Parsons and Stillwater. A different cruiser had come to replace the one on Mass Ave and was parked by the library on Tremont this time.

I was stiff and tired. My eyes felt as if they were half full of sand. My legs were heavy enough to sink a canoe - if I'd had one. I had a vision of me in a canoe paddling around alleyways full of water with herons flying past. Christ, I was getting woozy.

I decided to go back to the Johnson's and walked to where my car was parked. There were two tickets on it. Great.

When I climbed onto the driver's seat I closed my eyes for a second and could have been gone. There was a sort of humming torpor that enveloped me into which I could have sunk like a stone into warm water and been out for the morning. I forced myself to start the car and drove out of the South End.

A big white bruiser I'd never seen before opened the door at Linda's place. He didn't like my looks. I was probably looking pretty raunchy, if the truth were told. He was about to put the arm on me when Jonah came up the stairs with Linda ahead of him.

Linda ran to me and put her arms around me. She was just about to come undone. Jonah, grim-faced and tense as the cable on a ski lift, glowered at me, his huge fists opening and closing.

"Where is he, Jeeter?" Linda asked over and over. "Where is he?"

"We'll find him," I said. She felt good against me, but I gripped her shoulders and pushed her away. Her tear-streaked face lifted toward me and I could guess what horrors her imagination had presented to her in all this time, and how with every hour the fear, moving toward certainty, that Speedy must be dead had crept closer and closer.

We stepped into the livingroom, which was the spacious front room on the ground floor. A technician sat by the telephone, earphones on, a tape recorder at his side. The big white cop had come into the room with us.

"Are you one of Mooney's men?" I asked.

He said he was.

"No word yet?"

"Nothing."

There was a couch against the far wall. My legs eased me toward it without any conscious command from me. I remember sinking toward it. I think I was asleep before I lay down.

A blank. A bottomless hole. A blackness so complete I thought I would never come out of it. But an alarm was ringing. I opened my eyes. There was a blanket over me. The phone was ringing and Jonah was there. The technician nodded at Jonah and the latter lifted the receiver. "Hello," he said.

We could only guess at what was said at the other end of the line.

"Tha's right," Jonah said. "Okay. I go there at eleven this morning to sign the papers. They gonna have the title searched by then but I don't get no money until tomorrow."

There were words at the other end.

"Yeah," Jonah said. "Tha's awright. But I gotta hear my boy's voice before I bring the money. He ain't alive, you got nothin'."

More spluttering.

"Not good enough," Jonah said. "I gonna ask him one question. No way you can tape the answer in advance. He answer me right, I follow directions. He don't..."

Slowly, Jonah put the receiver back in the cradle. "Son of a bitch hung up," he said.

"You got it all?" the big cop asked.

"Every word," the technician said. He played the tape for us. There were no surprises. Rodrigues had asked if Jonah was the one who answered. Then he'd asked if he was getting the money from the bank. When Jonah said he wouldn't get the cash until tomorrow Rodrigues had said, "No bills bigger than fifties and all used." Jonah had said that was all right but he wanted to hear Speedy's voice. Rodrigues replied he'd let Speedy say Hello to him, but Jonah had insisted on asking Speedy a question. It was a smart move. Then Rodrigues cut the connection.

"Any chance of tracing the call?"

"Not enough time."

"Could you tell if it was local? Anything about what part of the city?"

"No chance."

"What about background noise? Did I hear some kind of roar - like a truck or a subway?"

"I think it was the sound of a subway," the technician said. "Maybe the El, because there was a horn sound too. Traffic noises."

I thought about that for a moment. The El runs along Washington Street for a long stretch. I hadn't prowled the whole length. And there was another place in Boston that came to mind where the subway came above ground. It was the Charles Street station at the bottom of Beacon Hill.

Rodrigues had made the call from a pay station - that was almost a certainty. Was he back on the Hill where so many of his other hideouts were located? Maybe I'd spent the night in the wrong locality.

Tony Morello had said that Speedy started back to the basement apartment where Chris died. He went back for the baseball Wade Boggs had autographed. But he didn't get it. Did Rodrigues grab him there, understanding that Speedy had decided to quit? If he did, he had to be holding Speedy somewhere close by. He couldn't have taken him any great distance against his will without being noticed.

I phoned Flo. She answered on the first ring.

"Have you found him yet?" she asked.

I told her I'd spent the night in the South End without doing any good but I was beginning to suspect Rodrigues was holding Speedy somewhere on the Hill.

"Are you all right?" I asked.

"I'm fine. I just wish you were here with me."

"I won't be long," I said.

I made a second call, this one to the Welfare Department, and gave them the name and address of Mrs. Rodrigues. Somebody would call on her in a day or two. I'd follow up on that to make sure.

It took half an hour to drive to Beacon Hill and find a parking place. At least I had a resident sticker for this area. Since I was parked on Pinckney Street, I went around the block to Myrtle and went into the building where Rodrigues had his own apartment.

Nothing was changed. It was just as I had left it. Anyone could walk in, but no one had. I wanted to be sure I hadn't seen a telephone there. Rodrigues was going to need to make at least one more call. The apartment might be a convenient place from which to make it. But there was no phone.

Next, I went to the building on Garden Street where the six boys had stayed. I got in without difficulty and went to the basement, but that apartment had been sealed off and padlocked by the police. No one was there.

On Hancock Street it was a different story. The front door had been jimmied. I walked in and went down to O'Leary's lair. Even before I reached his hole next to the boiler I knew something was wrong. I could smell it.

O'Leary lay on his face in a pool of vomit, but he wasn't drunk. He was dead. He'd been stabbed at least five times. Blood was still soaking into his shirt around each wound. Only on the edges had it begun to clot. He'd been dead only minutes. Of course he might have been dying for a while. Still, if it had been half an hour, more clotting would have occurred.

Just a little bit sooner and I would have had his murderer.

On the floor were short lengths of the same plastic-covered telephone wire I had found on Leroy. O'Leary's wrists and ankles were still tied. I looked to see if there was anything that could have been used as a gag and spotted two of them - old socks. They were lying on the floor. Someone else had been here with O'Leary. It had to have been Speedy. Rodrigues needed him alive - until he got the money. How had he taken him out of here? He'd untied him. The pieces of wire told me that. Was Speedy unconscious? Had he witnessed the stabbing of the helpless old man? That would be enough to give a lifetime of nightmares to even the most callous individual. How would it affect a sensitive fourteen-year-old? Maybe he'd fainted. But Rodrigues couldn't carry an unconscious kid around the streets without drawing attention.

I backed out of the boiler room and checked the rear door of the building. It was locked on the inside. No one went out that way.

I took the stairs two at a time and paused on each landing. Unless my radar was malfunctioning, there was no one in any apartment in the building.

Rodrigues had to have gone out the front way.

An east wind was bringing rain and cold in off the ocean. There were very few people out, but toward the top of the Hill I saw a postman go into a building. Fair weather or foul, he had to make his rounds. I caught him as he came out of the building and asked if he'd seen a black kid, probably in the company of a white man built like a professional wrestler.

He eyed me with suspicion. "Why do you want to know?"

I told him the boy had been kidnapped.

He didn't believe me.

I showed him my license and he looked at me again. "About fifteen minutes ago," he said. "They were walking down Revere Street. Arm in arm. The man didn't look queer. But you never know."

"How old was the kid?"

"How do I know? Young. Early teens. He loooked like he was sick. The man seemed to be holding him up."

That figured. If Speedy had been tied up and gagged for a day or more in the company of O'Leary, he would have been weak and hungry. And thirsty. Then if he'd watched Rodrigues stab O'Leary to death he could have gone into shock. So Rodrigues untied him, put an arm around him, maybe held a knife under his jacket inches from Speedy's ribs and walked him out into the November drizzle. Minutes later they'd been on Revere Street. Had Rodrigues found out where my building was? He'd been scouting the Hill for months, unless I was wrong, looking for places to rob. He could have had an eye on my place. Maybe one of the kids had told him about me. Or the Worcester cop?

I was running by then. If Rodrigues had used up all his hideouts it would be a bold move to go to my place. He'd know I had a phone. He might not know about Flo. Oh God, I thought, don't let him harm her.

The front door had been opened with a blade. I saw the marks on the wood the second I looked. I should have found a phone and called for help right then, but I wasn't thinking anymore. If that monster had reached Flo I wanted only to get my bare hands on him.

The elevator could have taken me to my top floor, but he'd have the door to the apartment covered, if he was there. I ran up to the second floor. The couple that lived in that one was never home before midnight. My key opened all the doors in the building. I went through the second floor apartment and stepped out onto the fire escape from the rear bedroom window and then climbed to my own level.

The rear window that gave access to the fire escape would have been easy to open quietly, the same way I'd entered Rodrigues's apartment on Myrtle Street, but someone had pushed one of my bookcases against it and had left the bookcase leaning inward, except for a string tied to the window latch. If I touched it the bookcase would fall and whoever was inside would know I was coming.

I could see over the top of the bookcase that the room, our bedroom, was empty. That meant that Rodrigues and Speedy and Flo were in the big front room on the street - unless he'd tied them and put them in the kitchen or the bathroom or a closet. And unless it wasn't Rodrigues at all.

My only hope was to take whoever it was by surprise. How would that be possible? There were no fire excapes on the front of the building, and there was no way to get to the front window except from above, or on a ladder from below. Neither way seemed feasible. But...

A year before I'd brought a sofa into the apartment by lifting it straight up from the rear patio. It was too long to fit in the elevator and too long for the winding stairs, but we'd hoisted it on a rope, removed the back window and slid it through the corridor to the livingroom. I had left the rope on the fire escape. It was still there, wrapped in plastic in case I might ever need it again.

I won't say it was as good as new, but it would easily bear my weight. I put the coil over my shoulder and went up the slate roof to the chimney. The fine drizzle falling made it slippery going. There was a thin growth of something like moss on some of the ancient shale. When I'd made a tight loop around the chimney and another around my waist, there was still enough line left to get me where I wanted to go, I hoped. Cautiously, I let out a foot at a time and walked backwards down the slimy slates to the front edge of the building.

Leaning outward, back to, I could see down the facade of my house to the brick sidewalk, the granite curb and the wrought iron spike of a lamp post some fifty feet below. Impaled on that, a body would be a pretty sight. I forced that image from my mind.

It was necessary to move two feet to my left so I wouldn't go over the edge in the middle of the window nearest me. I'd have to be able to look in without being seen. But suppose they were all in the kitchen? Or...

Better just hope and pray that Rodrigues would be where I could get a clean shot at him. I wouldn't be able to get my gun out of the holdster until I was firmly positioned at the side of the window with my left hand holding the rope.

I put one heel on the rim of the copper gutter and slid my other foot and ankle over the edge, groping for the brick facing of the building. From the ground, the overhang had always appeared to be a matter of inches.

My hands were sweating and as more and more of my weight went onto the rope, the strain began to tell on my fingers. I was all the way over the edge of the gutter, lying almost sideways, before my foot hit the bricks and I could pull my other leg over too. I suddenly wondered if there were any way I could get back up over the rim if I needed to. Better not think about that.

I took a deep breath and just then the edge of the gutter folded in with a snap. I didn't drop more than a few centimeters but it felt like a mile. My heart stopped. An icy sweat broke out all over me. I closed my eyes and counted to five, slowly. Eternity can be measured in microseconds.

Street noises were louder now that I was off the roof. Somebody, below, had spotted me and was calling to others to look. There was also the sound of a voice coming from inside my apartment. I couldn't make out what he was saying, but it was Rodrigues. He was speaking in clipped, rapid Spanish. Was someone else inside the place with him?

I walked several more careful steps backwards down the front of the building until my feet were level with the sill of the window. I looped the rope around my left wrist and gripped it tightly with that hand. It would soon cut off all circulation, but it gave me enough stability so I could use my right hand and get the gun from the holdster and click off the safety.

An inch at a time, I moved my head to the right and began peering into my front room. The first thing to come into view was the desk between the two front windows. Rodrigues's voice was clearer now and I realized he was on the phone to someone. That would give me an advantage, as long as he wasn't facing the window. The phone was on a small table near the door to the corridor, at the farthest point in the room from where I would see him.

I was holding the gun with the tip of the barrel almost touching my nose, my right arm close to my body. Leaning another inch to my right, I saw Flo tied and gagged in a straight-backed chair. She was looking toward the corridor, or toward Rodrigues perhaps.

One more inch and I saw Speedy, also tied to a chair. He hadn't noticed me either.

My left hand was going numb. I was beginning to shiver. The near-freezing rain was draining the heat out of me. With my right foot I groped for the window sill, found it, and eased myself far enough over so that I could see the whole livingroom.

Rodrigues was in the doorway to the corridor looking right at me, but for a split second he was staring into a middle distance the way you do when on the phone and concentrating on the words. He was quick, though, almost as quick as the single shot I got off through the double windows. I couldn't tell if I'd hit him. Ordinarily, I wouldn't have missed at fifteen feet, but two layers of glass would have deflected the shot.

He dropped the phone and was gone down the corridor. I kicked at the window and the storm sash shattered. At the same time, I heard a crash from the rear of the apartment and knew that Rodrigues had pulled over the bookcase and was getting onto the fire escape. If he was fleeing, I didn't have to worry, but if he'd seen I was hanging from a rope and he went to the roof and cut it I was going to be splattered all over Revere Street in about five seconds.

Desperately, I kicked at the inner window. It was a six-over six, built many years ago of sturdy stuff that only yielded, one mullion at a time, leaving jagged shards of glass along the edges.

Flo and Speedy, eyes bulging, helpless, watched as the seconds ran out on me. I couldn't kick away enough of the frame in the time I had left. Only one possibility remained. There were maybe eight feet from the gutter's edge to the loop around my paralyzed left hand. I pushed my gun through an opening in the window. It fell onto the floor. I grabbed the rope, then, in both hands, and kicked myself away from the building so that I swung four or five feet into the air over the street, turning myself as I arced outwards, and hunching over so that as I swung back I crashed like a cannon ball, butt first, into what was left of the casement. I landed on the floor, stunned, blood streaming down my cheek from a cut somewhere above my left eye. I was still clutching the rope but it was no longer attached to anything. It lay slack in my hands.

Flo and Speedy were both making throat noises, trying to warn me of something. Maybe they were saying Rodrigues's name. I pulled myself together, picked up the gun and crouched by the desk, ready to fire when he came back into the room.

But he didn't come back. We heard a clatter as he descended the fire escape. He was making a run for it.

I put the gun away and went to Flo. The second her gag was undone she said, "Quick, let me take care of that cut in your forehead."

I took time to kiss her once. It was a bloody slithery kiss, but she was unharmed and nothing else could ever matter as much as that. When she was free, she ran to the bathroom for first aid materials while I undid Speedy. There was terror in his eyes. He'd watched a boy die and seen a man stabbed to death and now here I was, leaning over him, dripping gouts of blood over him, after exploding through a window high over the street. He was going to need a lot of care if these specters were not going to haunt him all the rest of his life.

"Come in here," Flo called.

I stepped to the bathroom. She washed the gash above my eye and pressed a cold wet towel against it.

Speedy had followed me. He was trembling, but he was going to be all right.

"Pick up the phone," I told him, "and call your home. Tell them you're safe."

He went back to the livingroom. We heard him dial. Then we heard him say, "Momma, it's me. Yes." And after that he was crying, sobbing like the little kid he partly was, still close enough to childhood to be able to break down and let the tears flow without restraint. I held the compress in place and walked into the livingroom and took the phone out of his hands.

"Linda," I said. "Yes. Speedy's going to be fine. Flo is here too. At my place. We're all safe. Is Pat Mooney there?"

It wasn't Pat who got on the phone, it was the big cop from his office.

"We gotta call," he said. "Some loony is swingin' from chimney pots on Beacon Hill, smashin' windows, shootin' everyone in sight. Know anything about that?"

"I'll have to check it out later," I said. "But listen. Rodrigues is on the run. He's wounded, I think. He's only got about a two minute head start so he's still on the Hill. He'll have to hole up somewhere. And look. Get two men to the place on Hancock Street where O'Leary lived. O'Leary is there. Stabbed to death. And we've got an eye witness to the murder. You got that?"

"I'm already on it," he said, and hung up.

Flo covered my cut with a bandage and wound gauze around my head to hold it in place until I could get a doctor to sew it up. I was feeling unsteady so she went and got my car and drove the three of us to Speedy's house.

Linda was at the open door when we arrived. She stood there and Speedy ran to her. She put her arms around him and held him. In a few days he'd start resisting that closeness again, but for the moment it was what he most needed.

Jonah appeared beside them. Flo and I were standing, half way up the walk: Jonah didn't speak. He put one of his big paws on Speedy's head. The boy looked up at him, let go of his mother, and disappeared into his father's embrace. Andy was standing behind them.

We turned and got back into the car and drove away. We'd see them later, all four of them, but for the moment they needed to be with each other, alone in their own home without outsiders.

Flo took me to the Emergency entrance at MGH where I got my forehead properly stitched. Later, Mooney came to the apartment. Flo and I were in the kitchen having some chowder she'd prepared. She offered a bowl to Mooney but he refused.

"Thought you'd want to know we picked up Rodrigues," he said. "We cornered him in an alley off West Cedar Street. The bullet wound in his right thigh cut through some muscles on the outside of the leg and just nicked the femur. He was near collapse. No fight left in him."

Pat looked at the bandage on my head. "Lookin' a little peaked yourself. You get that when you were playin' Tarzan?"

"You should have seen him," Flo said. "The whole window was pulverized and he came through it from nowhere like some guided missile."

Pat shook his head. "He's a caution, ain't he?"

"I'll tell you something else, too," Flo said. "When Jeeter appeared at the window, Rodrigues was on the phone. He was setting up a way to rob Jonah of the money between the bank and his home so he wouldn't have to arrange for the transfer of ransom. My Spanish is rusty, but I could understand what he was planning. He was going to let Speedy say a couple of words to his father today. Then he was going to kill both of us and make his way to the place where they hoped to take Jonah by surprise in the morning."

"But then Jeeter broke up the phone conversation," Pat said, "and they must have known everything was coming apart." He rubbed his chin. "That would explain why the six men at El Honcho were so busy putting things in order when we busted in on them with a search warrant. Another fifteen minutes and we would have had nothing."

"Did you go through Station #4 to get the warrant?" I asked.

"I went over their heads," Pat said. "Had to, if we were gonna do any good. Even so, that detective named Bonaparte came in on us just after we got there. He'd found out somehow. We had 'cuffs on all the six guys in the place and were shakin' them down. 'Nice goin',' Bony says, like he was with us. I saw a couple of the Ricans look at him as if they didn't understand. There was still a lot of confusion. One guy was rollin' on the floor and kickin' anyone got near. I watched Bony in a mirror and when he thought no one could see him, he reached under a cooler and came up with a paper bag. He tucked it under his jacket.

"I turned around and put him against the wall. 'Lemme have it,' I said. He tried to give me some shit so I slapped him. He went for his gun. That time I decked him. Two of my men took his weapon and put 'cuffs on him. Then we pulled the bag out from under his jacket. It was the week's receipts.

"In the station, when we were bookin' the whole crew, one of them, name of Mario, who seems to be Mexican, said it was Bonaparte who shot the Worcester cop with his own gun. Then he gave the gun to one of the thugs at El Honcho. That was the gun you took off of him. I don't know if we can make it stand up in court, but we'll give it a try."

"What about the address on West Brookline Street?" I asked. "Has anybody been there yet?"

"Yeah. A team'll be there for days. You never saw so much stolen goods. That Rodrigues had too many things goin' for him. He couldn't keep up with them all."

33

It wasn't until two nights later that we saw Speedy again. Linda invited us for supper. Leroy was there, wearing a new suit. Even a tie and jacket. He didn't smile easily, but he was beginning to relax.

Speedy had on new slacks and a Norwegian hand-knitted sweater. He, too, had a serious air. He looked trim and handsome and grown up, but he stayed close to his mother and father.

The oldest person present was Mrs. Reese. Those ancient moist murky eyes of hers studied each of us in turn. She spoke little, but if there was anything she missed I can't guess what it could have been.

They'd put an extra leaf in the big kitchen table so that all eight of us could sit at it comfortably. Jonah, subdued but enormous, presided over the carving of the pork tenderloin and heaped extra portions of beet greens and potato and pork onto the plates of Speedy and Leroy.

"Gotta stuff these two turkeys so they don't fly away no more," he said.

Andy was seated next to Speedy. From time to time their eyes met. I saw Flo watching them. She was smiling.

For a while, after we'd all finished eating, we sat at the table, not saying much, just letting all that good food settle.

EAST FALMOUTH BRANCH

PLEASE DO NOT REMOVE
DATE DUE CARD FROM POCKET

By returning material on date due, you will help us save the cost of postage for overdue notices. We hope you enjoy the library. Come again and bring your friends!

FALMOUTH PUBLIC LIBRARY
Falmouth, Mass. 02540-2895
508-457-2555